# The King's Delight

SARAH HONEY

Copyright © 2023 by Sarah Honey.

All rights reserved. This book or any portion thereof may not be reproduced or used in any manner whatsoever without the express written permission of the publisher except for the use of brief quotations in a book review.

This is a work of fiction. Names, characters, business, events and incidents are the products of the author's imagination. Any resemblance to actual persons, living or dead, or actual events is purely coincidental.

Edited by Jennifer Smith for LesCourt Author Services.

Cover Art by Steph Westerik Illustration.

stephwesterik.com

ISBN: 9798367377811

# Dedication

*For Jen, who is to blame/thank for this whole thing. You're the best kind of bad influence.*

# Author's Note

The author has chosen to use UK English in this book.

# Contents

| | |
|---|---|
| Chapter 1 | 1 |
| Chapter 2 | 12 |
| Chapter 3 | 23 |
| Chapter 4 | 32 |
| Chapter 5 | 45 |
| Chapter 6 | 61 |
| Chapter 7 | 74 |
| Chapter 8 | 90 |
| Chapter 9 | 107 |
| Chapter 10 | 121 |
| Chapter 11 | 132 |
| Chapter 12 | 146 |
| Chapter 13 | 158 |
| Chapter 14 | 168 |
| Chapter 15 | 182 |
| Chapter 16 | 197 |
| Chapter 17 | 208 |
| Epilogue | 226 |
| *Afterword* | 237 |
| *About the Author* | 239 |
| *Also by Sarah Honey* | 241 |

## Chapter One

The man brandishing the staff was fast, but Felix was faster. He dodged the blow aimed at his midsection effortlessly, employing all the agility his lithe twenty-three-year-old frame possessed, but as he watched his opponent circle round again and saw the determined glint in the other man's eye, he knew that the time for finesse was past if he wanted to win. He ducked low and charged forward without warning, wrapping his arms around his opponent's waist and knocking him down before he had a chance to brace himself.

The man let out a grunt as his back hit the hard-packed dirt and his staff clattered to the ground, earning a whistle and a cheer from the members of the Royal Guard who had gathered to watch the pair spar. Felix forced the man's hands over his head and straddled his waist, pinning him in place. "Do you yield?" he demanded, his breath coming in short pants and the warm afternoon sun beating against the back of his neck.

His victim let out a low chuckle, his own breathing

laboured. "I yield. Now for the sake of all that's holy, let me up. I'm too old to be lying in the dirt." His light brown hair was threaded with silver and when he smiled, the lines in his face betrayed his age in a way his well-muscled physique didn't.

Felix grinned back and clambered up, standing and holding out a hand as those watching drifted away, leaving him alone with his father.

Janus Hobson grabbed hold and pulled himself to his feet, dusting himself off. "Good job, son. Any time you want to join the guard, there's a place for you."

Felix beamed at his father's approval. "Thanks, Dad. I still don't think the Royal Guard is the place for me, though."

"Are you sure? You'd be an asset."

Felix shook his head. "I was hired to work as the king's groom. That's what I'm trained for. I know you had dreams of me joining the guard and carrying on the family tradition but truly, I'd be terrible at it. I don't think I'm of the temperament to remain silent and keep watch over the royal arse."

His father gave a wry smile. "The correct term is His Majesty, King Leopold."

Felix shrugged. "You know I've never been good at observing formalities. Which is why, starting tomorrow, I have a job taking care of the royal horse's arse instead."

Janus snorted. "Maybe it's best if you can only offend the king's horse instead of the man himself." He reached up and ruffled Felix's hair like he was still a boy rather than a grown man, and Felix didn't begrudge him the gesture.

"I'm sure you'll do very well as the king's groom, son. And your mother and I are proud of you."

Felix beamed. Even though he didn't exactly need his father's reassurance, he appreciated it. "As long as I remember which end needs the feed bag and which the shovel, I can't make too big a mess of it, surely?"

His father laughed, their shoulders bumping as they walked from the packed-dirt training grounds together. Their footsteps left little puffs of dust in their wake. "You spent four years in Fortescue apprenticed under their head groom, and then you worked alongside him for another two. You're more than fit to take the position of the king's groom here. If you still can't tell one end of a horse from the other, either you had a terrible teacher or the horses in Fortescue are very different from ours."

In truth, the years of training in Fortescue had been long and gruelling. When Felix had received the invitation to come back home and work in the castle stables, he'd been glad of the chance, but he wouldn't trade the experience he'd gained while he was away. He truly did adore working with horses. He loved the magnificence of them—their sheer size and strength, the sleek muscles and glossy flanks, the wide eyes that seemed to stare into his very soul. Getting a horse to trust him and follow his commands always felt like a victory and a conspiracy all at once—he and his mount, joined in silent accord. He'd worked hard to learn as much as he could, and during his time in training, he'd taken every bit of advice given to him by other more experienced grooms, carving out a reputation for himself as an excellent horseman in the process.

An unexpected benefit of leaving Lilleforth had been

the freedom of not being pigeonholed as "the captain of the guard's son" and having his actions reported back to his father. That alone had more than made up for the early mornings, backbreaking labour, and literal mountains of horseshit that he'd dealt with on a daily basis.

It had also meant that when he'd finally acknowledged it wasn't the cleavage on the kitchen maids that made his heart beat faster but the gentle curve of another stable boy's arse—which hadn't been *that* much of a revelation—he'd been free to explore the possibilities without worrying that someone would tell tales. Not that he'd thought his parents would mind, at least he'd *hoped* not, but a young man was entitled to some privacy, after all.

He'd gotten to explore those inclinations in all their glory a few months after he'd arrived in Fortescue as a fresh-faced lad of seventeen. Up until then he'd kept what he liked to himself, unsure how one even went about finding someone with the same desires as him. But that had changed when a visiting stable master had caught Felix's gaze lingering on the cut of his riding trousers a moment too long. The man had sidled up to him and, with a wink and a smile, invited Felix for what he'd called "a stroll in the meadow."

There had been a meadow, certainly, but very little strolling. There *had* been a lot of rolling, some writhing, and a lot of desperate panting culminating in an absolutely spectacular buggering that had driven any thoughts of ever bedding a maid from Felix's mind forever.

By the time the stable master left Fortescue at the end of two weeks, Felix had learned a lot of things that had nothing at all to do with equine care, although there *had* been a riding crop involved one memorable evening. Felix had been both shocked and thrilled to discover that when it was a lover brandishing the crop, it was *nothing* like when his father had put Felix over his knee as a boy, and that in the bedroom, he relished the sweet slap of leather against his skin.

Felix took every opportunity to practice his new skills after that, and by the end of his six years in Fortescue, he was quite the expert when it came to giving and receiving a good rogering—along with a spanking—whenever his favorite stable master came to visit.

One of the stable boys had even shed a tear when he said goodbye, and Felix would have been touched except for the fact that the lad had been cradling Felix's spit-damp cock when he'd whispered, "I'll miss you."

Yes, one could say his education in Fortescue had been thorough on all fronts.

As he walked now, shoulder to shoulder with his father as they crossed the cobbled courtyard of the castle, Felix found himself wondering if he'd be able to have the same kind of adventures here. Surely now that he was a grown man, there was no need for stories to be carried back to his father? It was part of the reason he hadn't joined the Royal Guard in the first place. He knew himself well enough to know that he'd itch and chafe under the weight of his father's benevolent supervision, no matter how well intentioned it was. At least working in the stables, he'd have a measure of freedom—unless the king was prowling around, of course.

Felix still had no idea whether the king rode or not. He didn't know whether he ever made his way to the stables or even what the man looked like up close. By design, Felix hadn't seen the then-crown prince, except in passing, since he'd been a boy of twelve and his father had still called him Flick. Felix's mouth had always run to trouble, and his parents had thought it wise for him to steer clear of all persons royal and potentially offendable after the time he'd failed to recognise the prince and inadvertently called him a stuck-up little tit. There had been a grudging apology and some grovelling, but after that, throughout his teenage years and beyond, Felix had made himself largely invisible where Prince Leopold was concerned.

Oddly enough, that hadn't prevented him from forging a kind of friendship with the prince's closest confidant, Mattias—Chancellor Allingdon—which was how he'd come to land the job as the king's groom. Felix was fairly certain that Mattias had forgotten that he had insulted Leopold long ago, although it was also possible that he remembered and had hired Felix because of it.

Still, Felix had no clue what kind of man he'd be dealing with. He hoped that the king wasn't a man who was cruel to his horses, or Felix might not be able to hold his tongue if he encountered it.

"Does Leo ride," he asked his father, "or does he only have a horse for the look of the thing?"

"It's *King Leopold*," his father said with a sigh, "or Your Majesty or sire, and you'd best not forget it."

"Well, obviously I'm not calling him Leo to his face, am I? If he's like any of the other royals I met while I was away, he's probably got a stick fair up the royal arse."

Janus chuckled. "Oddly enough, he only has a stick up his rear end when it comes to the care of his horse. And in answer to your question, he'd ride every day if given the chance. He absolutely adores being on horseback. You and he are alike in that way, at least."

Relief spread through Felix. A man who loved horses couldn't be *too* much of an arse, surely? As long as Felix remembered his manners around him, he'd be fine.

As if reading his thoughts, his father patted his shoulder. "Keep a hold of your tongue and take good care of Blackbird, and you'll get along fine."

"Blackbird?"

"The king's mount. She's a gorgeous great thing, black as a raven and sweet as a nut, and he's besotted with her. Guard that horse with your very life, son." He hesitated. "Of course, when I say guard her with your life, I'm speaking as the captain of the guard. As your *father,* I say if someone wants to take her badly enough and you're in danger, let them have her. The king can always get another mount, but I only have one son."

Felix swallowed the lump in his throat. "Thanks, Dad. I'll try and remember that if I encounter any vicious-looking horse thieves."

"See that you do. I want to see you grow old, settle down, and find yourself a nice lass," Janus said, and something about the way his eyebrows were raised made the comment feel very much like an invitation to tell his father the thing that Felix suspected he already knew.

He swallowed again. "About that..."

His father stayed silent, and Felix knew he was waiting, doubtless aware that Felix regarded silence as an enemy to be bludgeoned to death under the sheer weight of words.

"I don't think I'm inclined to lovely lasses, actually."

It wasn't all *that* uncommon for like to be attracted to like, and most people didn't seem to care what other people did in bed, but it wasn't something Felix had ever explicitly shared with his father either. He stared at the ground as he walked, his chest tight.

Janus gave a noncommittal hum, and when he spoke there was no judgment in his tone. "I had wondered. A good-looking boy like yourself, living in a kingdom the size of Fortescue, yet your letters never once held any mention of romance." Felix risked a sideways peek and found his father regarding him with a soft look. "It's all right, son. You're in good company." Janus lowered his voice. "Royal company, if the stories are to be believed."

Felix almost stumbled over his own feet at that. "How do you know that?" he asked, intrigued. "Has the king said—"

His father chuckled. "Nobody has said a word. The castle staff have been the very soul of discretion, as they always are when it comes to lovers. But I didn't become the captain of the guard by failing to see what's in front of my face. And the fact is the king has turned down seven marriage proposals from princesses in surrounding kingdoms in the past two years since he took the throne."

"That doesn't mean anything, though."

"Not on its own, no. But very occasionally I've admitted young men to the castle for private meetings with His Majesty, and I do not believe that there is any business so urgent that it needs to be discussed in the king's bedchamber at midnight."

"There might be other reasons. Maybe it's espionage and he's meeting his spies." Felix wasn't sure why he found it so hard to believe that the king held the same inclinations as him, but even considering it made his heart flutter in his chest.

"Yes," his father said drily. "Jim, the baker's lad, is highly trained in espionage. That must be it."

That startled a laugh out of Felix. They approached the small side door to the castle that led in through the wet room and laundry area to the kitchens. "Fine. Your explanation makes more sense."

It was cool inside the stone walls, the shade a welcome relief from the midday sun, and Felix and his father both splashed cold water on their faces at the washbasins that were set on a wooden trestle for just that purpose. Janus wiped the sweat from the back of his neck with a damp cloth. "You keep what I've told you quiet, mind," he said. "Not because it's wrong, but because it's nobody's business but the king's."

Felix nodded. He *could* be discreet when the occasion called for it. Felix had no desire to jeopardise his father's position by failing to hold his tongue. Besides, if anyone could appreciate the freedom a little privacy afforded, it was him. Still, he was glad he'd shared with his father today. It meant that if whispers *did* get back to him about Felix bedding the occasional lad around the castle, at least his father wouldn't be too surprised.

"Are you moving into your cottage today?" His father's voice pulled him from his thoughts.

Felix nodded. "I'll finish moving my things after lunch and then spend the afternoon with the horses." Felix's new position as the king's groom came with his own small cottage adjacent to the stables, and after six years of bunking in shared quarters at Fortescue, he was looking forward to the privacy.

"And when are you meeting the king?"

Felix made a face. "Matty said—"

"You mean His *Excellency*—"

Felix rolled his eyes. "Fine! *His Excellency, Chancellor Mattias Allingdon,* says he'll arrange something next week, but that Leo—His *Majesty*, I'm *trying*, all right?—is snowed under for the rest of this week with some sort of quarterly meetings. But Matty also said there's no rush because Leopold won't have time to ride this week anyway."

His father was obviously fighting to hold back laughter. "You really do struggle with titles, don't you?"

"I swear, they'll be the death of me." Felix let out a frustrated sigh. "Maybe when I meet the king, I'll just nod and smile and stay silent."

His father did laugh then. "I'm remembering now why we kept you away from King Leopold when he was still only a prince." He patted Felix's shoulder in a comforting gesture. "Try not to worry, son. As long as you take good care of Blackbird, I suspect the king will forgive you anything. And Felix? It's good to have you back."

He pulled Felix into a rough hug, and Felix returned it wholeheartedly.

It was good to *be* back.

Felix was looking forward to settling into his new position, getting to know the horses and the other grooms, and being able to see his family more often than his previous annual visits to Ravenport had allowed.

And from a personal viewpoint, now that he was home

for good, Felix was in a place to entertain the possibility of maybe finding someone for more than a casual stroll in the meadow. While he'd enjoyed sowing his wild oats over the past few years, waking up next to a different body every morning was losing its thrill, and he was starting to yearn for something more than a fling.

Felix knew that, objectively, he was attractive. His past lovers had praised his long limbs and lean build, his honey-gold eyes and long lashes. There had even been a hasty, filthy ode composed by a lusty bard that sang the praises of his soft skin and thick, dark hair, and how perfect it was for tangling fingers in during a quick rut against a wall. He'd been told he had a mouth made for kisses and sin.

And that was all well and good, but surely there must be more? What he really wanted was to find someone with shared interests that went beyond the physical.

Surely, in a city the size of Ravenport, there must be at least one available man who'd find him attractive *and* intelligent, someone who would look past his surface good looks and see the person underneath…someone who was willing to while away more than a single evening with him? Perhaps there might even be someone who worked at the castle.

He could only hope.

## Chapter Two

"I don't *want* to." Leopold, King of Lilleforth, pouted and sat back in his ornate desk chair with a huff. He folded his arms across his broad chest just in case his long-suffering Chancellor Mattias was in any doubt about exactly how much Leopold didn't want to sit through an entire day of meetings. "They don't really care about what I have to say anyway. I'm just a figurehead in most of these matters. You know that."

Mattias gave a sigh, one that seemed to have been dragged directly from the soles of his boots, and pinched the bridge of his nose. "Exactly," he said in resigned tones that spoke of having had a similar conversation countless times before. "You're His Majesty King Leopold Augustus Salisbury, reigning monarch of Lilleforth. You're known for being approachable, a man of the people, who oversees his kingdom with a firm but fair hand. And you know very well that part of that is you personally overseeing the quarterly budget and administration meetings. So stop pouting, put your boots back on, and pretend you give a damn.

They'll be here in ten minutes, and you'd better have stopped sulking like a stroppy child by then and be prepared to give these people the attention that they need and deserve."

Leopold gave the man a narrow look but Mattias remained unmoved, as Leopold had known he would. His chancellor was his best friend and a necessary thorn in his side, and Leopold wouldn't be without him—except for times like this when Mattias insisted that Leopold fulfil his role properly.

It was many years since a seventeen-year-old Mattias Allingdon had found a lost fourteen-year-old Prince Leopold wandering the woods and returned him home, but Leopold still remembered it vividly. He'd thought that his rescuer had hung the moon, and it was also the first time he'd felt the stirrings of attraction for a boy—confirmation that while his future might hold a princess or a noblewoman, there was definitely room for dalliances with a dashing young man or two along the way.

And perhaps it had been selfish, but Leopold had begged—demanded, really, with all the arrogance of youth and privilege—that his father do something to keep his interesting new friend around.

And because Leopold was the prince, of course he'd gotten his own way. At least, that was what he'd thought at the time. Looking back now, he reflected that his father's acceptance of his demands had been far more calculated and pragmatic than he'd realised at the time.

Leopold's mother had passed away when he was only two, and he'd been raised by nannies and nursemaids for as long as he could remember, but at fourteen he'd been something of a handful—too old for the nursery, too young for court. So when he'd taken a shine to Mattias, his father, who had been grateful to have his wandering progeny returned in one piece, had seen an opportunity to keep his son in check while giving him the illusion of freedom. He'd offered Mattias a position as Leopold's companion, practically begging him to stay.

Mattias had jumped at the chance. It was some years later that he'd told Leopold he would have taken any opportunity to escape his drunken father and poverty-stricken home life.

And although their relationship had never developed into anything more than friendship, Leo and Mattias *were* friends, the two of them as thick as thieves. Upon finding that Mattias was both trustworthy and level-headed, Leopold's father had been thrilled and had put plans in motion for the boy's future.

Mattias had received further schooling as well as hand-to-hand combat training, and once he was proficient, he was appointed Leopold's personal bodyguard. The two boys had remained glued to each other's side as they grew older, getting each other into and out of trouble in equal measure. Mattias, though, was always the voice of reason, and thus had been steadily rising through the ranks in the years since. He'd been helped along by the education he'd received, which had encompassed all the areas of royal protocol, diplomacy, and strategic planning that the future king's right-hand man might need to know, because the king was no fool.

Mattias was knighted on his twenty-first birthday at Leopold's request, and one of the first things Leopold had done upon ascending to the crown two years ago had been to appoint Mattias to the position of chancellor. There was nobody Leopold trusted more—which didn't make it any less irritating when Mattias was right.

Leopold gave his own sigh and bent down beneath the desk to wrestle his footwear back on, grumbling under his breath about power-hungry little upstarts. When he emerged from under the desk, Mattias looked him up and down before getting out of his chair and walking round to Leopold's side of the desk. He crouched in front of his king, straightening his collar and smoothing his hair until Leopold batted his hand away. "I assume you won't be wearing your coronet today?"

"You just said I'm a man of the people, so no," Leopold said, savouring the petty triumph. He hated his coronet—it was uncomfortable, and it felt like any sudden move would send it toppling—and found any excuse he could to avoid wearing it. It wasn't an argument he always won, but today it seemed he had the victory.

Mattias threw him a rueful smile. "As you wish. I'll go and see if they're ready for us, *Your Majesty*."

Leopold screwed up his nose at the use of his official title, but he knew why Mattias had done it. It was a gentle reminder that it was time to fall into his public persona, that of Lilleforth's all-knowing, benevolent king, rather than a thirty-two-year-old man who had no time for unnecessary pomp and ceremony, who would rather be out riding his horse, and who still grumbled whenever he had to wear his boots indoors.

Leopold huffed, fidgeted with his collar, and settled himself with his hands clasped loosely on his desktop, leaning slightly forward and giving every appearance of an interested, engaged leader. "Go on then, send them in."

The sooner they started, the sooner they'd be done, and if Leopold played his cards right, maybe he'd be able to persuade Mattias to go riding with him this afternoon.

Several endless hours later Leopold watched the retreating back of his housekeeper, and when he was sure she was gone and the door had closed behind her, he let out a groan and slumped forward, his head hitting the desk with a loud thunk. "Are we done?"

"We're done."

He didn't need to look up to know that Mattias was rolling his eyes.

"Thank the gods," Leopold said with a sigh, lifting his head. He hated the quarterly review meetings, even though he knew they were necessary. "I've never been so bored in all my life. Why do I even need to know how many pounds of flour we've used this month? I feel like I've been in this office for days—no, *weeks*. Maybe I'll go riding, get some fresh air."

Mattias nodded. "I'm not free, but let me arrange a squadron of guards and—"

"Nooooooo, not with the guards, it'll be no fun." Leopold's head thunked against the desk again. "Ow."

Mattias snorted. "That's what you get for being dramatic."

Leopold narrowed his eyes. "Are you showing disrespect to your king, Chancellor?"

"Definitely, Majesty," Mattias said, plopping down in the chair opposite Leopold and extending his long legs to drop his feet on the desk. The *royal* desk. "Are you planning to do anything about it?"

"I might," Leopold grumbled, but they both knew it was a lie. Mattias was his best friend, and Leopold would be lost without him. *Still,* Leo thought, *he could at least* pretend *to have some sort of respect*. "Are you sure I can't go for a quick gallop by myself?" he asked, hoping against hope.

"If you ride, you need guards, Leo," Mattias said, arching an eyebrow. "Riding alone is too risky."

"But if I take the guards, it won't be a ride, it'll be a *show,* and all the little sycophants will crowd around and I'll have to walk my horse sedately and *behave*," Leopold grumbled, that long-buried spoiled teenager rearing to the surface for a moment. He just wanted to ride—to race across green grass, breathe deeply and get some fresh air in his lungs, and feel the wind in his hair. It didn't seem like too much to ask. "Why can't I go alone just this once? A ride will relax me after the morning I've had."

"Yes, because an assassination attempt is always a soothing way to spend an afternoon," Mattias said drily.

"I'm the king. I could order you to let me ride."

"You could, certainly. But I've grown somewhat fond of you over the years, and I'd rather not see you murdered. No guards, no ride." He gave Leopold a look that dared him to disagree.

Leopold sighed, shoulders slumping, and dropped his head back onto the desk, more gently this time. After a moment he turned to find Mattias watching him, wearing the smug air of someone who had won their latest battle. "Anyway, what do you mean you're *somewhat* fond of me?" he muttered. "You adore me as your king, surely?"

Mattias grinned, showing even white teeth. "As your subject? I'm devoted to you. As your friend who's known you for over half your life? You're tolerable—when you're not being a stubborn arse."

"I should have sent you back to your father as a teenager," Leopold muttered.

"And I should have left you crying in the woods when you were a lost brat, yet here we are."

Leopold made a show of rolling his eyes, but he couldn't help his smile at the familiar teasing. His and Mattias's bickering had long since had any sharp edges smoothed out through years of affectionate repetition.

Mattias took his feet off the desk and sat up straight. "As your chancellor *and* your friend, I'd advise that you get started on that pile of official correspondence. I'm fairly certain there are several marriage proposals in there, and if you ignore them for much longer, the senders will start to assume that the lack of a no indicates an acceptance."

Leo screwed up his nose. "Why do other kingdoms *insist* on throwing princesses at me? They must know I'm going to say no by now."

"They *throw princesses at you* because not only does Lilleforth have a port and coastal access, but you also hold strategic alliances with the other two most powerful kingdoms on the continent. The royal advisors assume that you'll have to marry eventually, so it makes sense that they might as well put their candidate forward and hope for the best. Besides," he added, "you're not unattractive."

That much, Leopold knew, was true. He'd been blessed with a pleasant countenance that featured piercing blue eyes, a strong jaw, a fine, straight nose, and thick, glossy hair that was so black it almost looked blue in the sunlight. Leo had no desire to be one of those squat, round kings, and so he made certain to keep himself fit. He spent time outdoors riding, training with the guards, chopping wood, and lifting bales of hay in the stables, which resulted in a well-muscled physique, and he was justifiably proud of it. It was certainly effective when wooing an attractive lad.

Still, he felt vaguely annoyed at his physical attractiveness being used as a selling point. "I feel like a prize steer on the auction block," he grumbled.

"And you think those poor girls don't? Just imagine the indignity of being presented as a marriage candidate and knowing you'll be refused, just because your potential husband is also the realm's most confirmed bachelor."

"That's you, surely?" Leopold teased.

Mattias quirked a crooked smile. "My reasons for not taking a bride are quite different to yours, as you well know. The woman I marry needs to be extraordinary, purely because when she marries me, she gets *you* by proxy—and you'd stretch any wife's patience." He ran a hand through messy golden hair that was showing the barest hint of silver at the temples.

"Have I mentioned your total and utter lack of respect today?"

"Several times. Have I mentioned that you really must deal with that correspondence?" Mattias stood and stretched, making himself appear even taller than he already was, and walked toward the door. "And *no riding*."

It was almost as if he thought Leopold couldn't be trusted.

"Fine," Leopold muttered. "I'll do the paperwork. But I don't want to see anyone for the rest of the day."

Mattias gave Leopold a nod, pausing with one hand on the door handle. "We can go riding tomorrow, just the two of us," he conceded. "I'll make time."

"Not today?" Leopold gave his best wide-eyed look, the one that had persuaded a variety of young men to come tumbling into his bed over the years.

Mattias ignored it, immune after half a lifetime. "Not today. I have work to do, and you have far too much correspondence to ignore it any longer. It won't kill you to wait until tomorrow."

Easy for him to say.

After Mattias had taken his leave, Leopold heaved a resigned sigh and flicked through the important but mind-numbing paperwork that was stacked on his desk in an accusing pile.

There were, indeed, several proposals. They weren't *presented* as proposals, of course. There was an etiquette to these things. One was an invitation to a ball in a neighbouring kingdom to celebrate the princess's coming of age, and one was a letter informing him that Princess Sophia, heir to the throne of Evergreen, was traveling his way. It came with an invitation to host her and her retinue for a week while she passed through Lilleforth, which of course came with the unspoken assumption that Leopold would host a banquet for his royal guests.

Leopold tipped his head back and gave a long exhale. Turning down the first invitation was easy enough, but the second one was trickier. He had no good reason to refuse visitors, and it would be nothing short of a slap in the face not to host an event to welcome his guests. Leo had to hand it to whoever was in charge at Evergreen; they were clever. It looked like just this once, Leopold might have to actually meet the princess he was planning on rejecting.

Princess Sophia was older than many of the princesses who sought to court Leopold, having reached her mid-twenties unwed. She had a reputation for dismissing her suitors out of hand, much like Leopold did. He could only assume that, also like him, she was under pressure to find a suitable partner—and Leopold was eminently suitable, even if he did say so himself.

Leopold put the letter to one side to discuss with Mattias later.

He ploughed through half the pile of correspondence, but his heart wasn't in it and his concentration wandered. Eventually, after reading the same paragraph four times and failing to make head or tail of it, he threw down the document and stood, pacing up and down restlessly as he ruminated on the unfairness of it all. He was the head of the *entire country* and perfectly capable of looking after himself, yet here he was confined to the castle and forced to write letters as if he were a naughty child with unfinished lessons.

Well, he'd never stayed in his rooms for lessons when he was a child either, and the one time he *had* gotten lost, it had turned out perfectly fine. Better than fine, even, because he'd gotten Mattias out of it.

Did a king *really* need permission from his chancellor to go riding on his own lands?

No, Leopold decided. He didn't.

He was the king, and he didn't need permission or guards just to go out for an hour or two and clear his head. If he wanted to go riding, he'd go, regardless of what that mother hen Mattias had to say about it.

Still, he made sure the coast was clear before he slipped out of his office.

## Chapter Three

Felix wiped the sweat from his brow with a rag, rolled his neck, and then tipped the last two buckets into the horse troughs, which were now filled with fresh, clear water. The stone sides had been scrubbed clean, and they were free of all traces of the slime and muck that inevitably gathered.

"Since when does the king's groom take care of the troughs? That's what the lads are for."

Felix turned to find the stable master, Mother Jones, leaning against the fence and watching him with a raised eyebrow. Mother—there'd been some sort of a mix-up on his birth certificate, apparently—was somewhere in his late forties, all long and lean and whipcord muscle that spoke of a lifetime of hard work. He had been the stable master for approximately forever and Felix had fond memories of his own time as a junior stable hand working under the man.

It was Mother who, at Mattias's request, had arranged for Felix's placement in Fortescue. The man was devoted to his horses and good at his job, although it seemed that wrangling their newest hire, Davin, was proving to be something of a challenge. Davin often disappeared for hours at a time, and no matter how often he was told an honest day's work wouldn't kill him, he didn't seem inclined to take the risk.

Felix shrugged. "I've already taken care of Blackbird and Shadow and the water was getting low. Ollie's out working with the yearling and Davin's wandered off again, so it was easier to do the job myself than try and track the little bugger down."

Mother threw his head back and gazed at the heavens as if praying for strength. "Slack little shit. When I find him, I'm sending him to you, and you can give him something to do that'll make him regret dodging his duties."

Felix grinned. "I'm sure there's a pile of shit somewhere that needs shovelling."

Mother's answering smile showed off crooked teeth. "There's always shit that needs shovelling."

"I recall a pile that Davin was meant to move the day before yesterday, and it's been uncommonly warm," Felix said, "so it should be properly ripe. He can start with that."

Mother hummed and gave a nod. "I swear, that boy doesn't seem to know one end of a shovel from the other, but I'm sure with enough practice he'll figure it out."

Technically Felix held no power over the stable boys, but in practical terms, he was the king's groom, and the position carried an innate sort of authority. On Felix's first day there, Mother had told the lads that they were to obey any orders from Felix as if they came from Mother himself.

Then he'd told Felix to feel free to give the lads a clip around the ears if he caught them shirking.

Felix had nodded, even though he had no intention of clipping any ears—well, not unless it was really and truly deserved.

Hells, it wasn't that he didn't understand the desire to slack off. It didn't seem that long since he was sixteen himself, and he'd been guilty of sneaking away for the afternoon more than once. The difference between him and Davin, though, was that he'd always, always made sure he'd completed his tasks first. Then again, Davin was barely fifteen, and it wasn't that he was lazy so much as he was easily distracted, and as Mother had mentioned, he genuinely seemed clueless. Felix was confident that, given time and enough shovelling, they'd get Davin to realise that the animals were reliant on him for their basic needs, and that would motivate him to do his job.

At least nobody was relying on the stable lads to take care of the king's horse—that job was Felix's alone, and he did it gladly.

Based on the last few days, he could see himself settling into his role well enough. His cottage was well appointed, far nicer than anywhere he had stayed in Fortescue, he got along with Mother and the lads, and best of all, in Felix's opinion, was the bond he was starting to build with the king's horse, Blackbird.

The king's mount had her own separate stable which she shared with Shadow, the grey gelding who was her companion horse and who had taken a liking to Felix immediately. The feeling was mutual.

It hadn't been quite as easy with Blackbird, but after

several days spent getting acquainted, Blackbird seemed to have accepted Felix as someone to be trusted, and now her head lifted and she let out a happy sound whenever Felix came into view. Of course, her affection could have been based purely on the fact that he always made sure to bring her an apple or a carrot when he came to see her, but Felix liked to think that she recognised him as a man of good character rather than just a source of treats.

Blackbird really did have a sweet nature, as Felix had discovered when taking her out in the mornings for her exercise. The first time he'd ridden her he'd been…not nervous, exactly, but aware that their relationship was new, so he'd made sure to start off slow, walking her sedately across the cobbled courtyard and giving her the chance to get a feel for the weight of him. But when they'd left the castle compound and she'd caught sight of the green fields in front of her, she'd huffed once, a shiver of restrained impatience running through her, and he'd *known* that she wanted to run.

Once he'd let her have her head, she'd proved an absolute joy to ride—fast, certainly, but also responsive, allowing Felix to guide her along the worn tracks that ran through the long grass without pulling on the reins even once. It was then that Felix had decided that if staying in His Majesty's good graces meant sometimes getting to ride Blackbird, then even if upon meeting the king he discovered him to be an absolute twat, he'd still be on his politest behavior.

In truth, Felix was somewhat surprised that he hadn't seen the king yet. His father had assured him that Leopold loved to ride, but it had been a week and Felix still hadn't met him. Although there *were* those quarterly reports that Mattias had told him about, so maybe it wasn't so surprising.

And it did mean that he had the pleasure of riding Blackbird most mornings. They'd started to go farther afield, and as far as Felix was concerned there was no more invigorating feeling in the world than galloping over open ground and through wooded trails with the crisp morning air fresh on his face as he rode for long miles, only turning back when the sun rose higher in the sky and Blackbird slowed to a trot, letting him know that she was ready to go home. Felix didn't know how the king could own such a wonderful beast and not ride her every single day.

"His Majesty must be itching to go for a ride by now," Mother said, as though reading his thoughts.

"Oh?" Felix patted at the damp skin of his arms with some rough towelling before draping it over the wooden railing enclosing the yard.

"Aye. He doesn't normally go this long without getting a leg over."

Felix smirked and raised an eyebrow. "Is that so? I'd heard stories."

"His *horse*, without getting a leg over his *horse*." Mother sputtered, and Felix laughed. "Little shit." Mother threw a wet rag at Felix, who caught it, still laughing.

It did remind him of something he'd meant to ask about, though. "Is it true what they say about the king?"

"Well, it depends," Mother said with a wry smile. "Are you talking about the rumour that His Majesty is smarter than he lets on and has a plan for every circumstance, or the one where he's nothing but a pretty man with an empty head and the chancellor's the one who runs the kingdom? Maybe you mean the tale that he'll bed anyone with a pulse —or perhaps that he's never been kissed?"

"Oh." Felix hadn't realised there was such a selection. "Um…"

It was Mother's turn to laugh. "There's not a king born who doesn't have tales told about him. But I feel that you *actually* mean the one where he prefers a fine manly chest and a set of bollocks to a buxom wench?"

Felix swallowed. "That…yes."

"I don't know about the other stories, but that one has some truth to it. He's discreet about it, but he's had a lover or two over the years. And he's charming enough that he doesn't have any trouble finding willing bedmates." He gave a soft smile. "Truth be told, I'm rather fond of His Majesty, even if he can be an arse at times."

Felix sighed as he leaned against a stable door and folded his arms over his chest. "You call him an arse, yet you insist on using his title."

"Aye, well. It's about respect, isn't it? It's important, showing the proper respect." Mother ducked his head in a tiny bow, and Felix wasn't sure he even knew he was doing it. "He's the *king*, after all."

"Even if he's an arse?"

"Even if he's *sometimes* an arse," Mother said. He tilted his head. "You must remember the king, lad. You grew up here."

He shrugged. "Let's just say that given my mouth's tendency to run on, after I insulted Leopold once, it was decided that it was in my best interests not to be wherever he was. I haven't seen him since I was twelve."

"Ah," Mother said, eyes sparkling with mirth. "You called him names, I remember now. I'd forgotten that."

"Let's just hope he has as well," Felix said as they both walked into the stable. "Hopefully, he won't recognise me as the boy who insulted him."

Mother hummed. "You look nothing like the skinny little whelp you were as a child. I think you're safe."

"I was not a skinny little whelp!"

"You were," Mother said with a grin. "You were built almost entirely of elbows and ribs." He looked Felix up and down, appraising. "Not anymore, though. You've grown into a fine young man. If I were you, I'd take advantage of that and find yourself some company in the evenings. I'm sure there are plenty who'd be willing to help you sow your wild oats." Mother's smile widened. "Oh, that's a good one! Oats, right? Because you're a groom." He prodded a nearby sack of feed with his boot just in case Felix had missed his meaning. "Oats, right? Feed?" He might have carried on in that vein indefinitely, but his attention was caught by something outside the door, and the next minute he was striding across the stable and out into the yard, bellowing as he went. *"Davin!* Where the blazes have you been?"

As the sound of shouting and Mother's boots on the cobblestone receded, Felix fiddled idly with a set of reins that were looped over Blackbird's stall and thought about what Mother had said. The problem was he didn't *want* to sow any more wild oats. He'd done plenty of that. No, he was ready for something more settled in his life. But it wasn't like someone was just going to fall into his lap, was it?

Perhaps he should just be satisfied with his casual liaisons for now. After all, he was good-looking enough and could be charming when the occasion called for it, and there was no denying that he was a talented lover. What was a one-time thing for him might turn out to be the night of his partner's life, and really, it would be churlish of him to keep his talents to himself when there was an entire city of men out there, at least some of them desperate for cock.

Besides, Felix *did* love a tumble in the sheets, and he suspected he'd miss it if he gave it up completely. Maybe he'd continue to sow his oats after all, and if he was lucky, what started as a casual dalliance might grow into something more.

He just had to find a willing soul to dally with.

He was pulled from his thoughts by the movements of a slow-moving figure slinking across the yard—and whoever this was, they *were* slinking. They had a battered, wide-brimmed hat pulled down low over their face and they were progressing at a snail's pace, pressing their back against any available wall and pausing before almost gliding to the next bit of wall.

Felix stood out of sight inside the stable doors and watched, intrigued. Was it a spy? An assassin? Someone sneaking away to meet a lover? Or was this just an adult version of Davin, someone skiving off from his duties? Whoever it was, as they got closer, Felix was able to make out that it was a grown man, tall and well-built, and his attention was captured by the man's deliciously thick neck. Despite his face being obscured, Felix felt drawn to the stranger, enchanted by both his solid musculature and his almost feline manner of gliding forward.

Perhaps it was because he'd just been thinking about such things, but Felix couldn't help but wonder if the man would make the same lithe, catlike movements if Felix were to take him to bed and whether he'd crawl up the mattress while wearing a wicked smirk. He poked his head out the door a fraction to see better in the hopes of catching a glimpse of the stranger's face, and it was then that he realised the man was heading straight for the stables.

He ducked back inside, mind racing. Should he clatter about a bit to make his presence known and give him the chance to change course? Or should he stay hidden and see what he was up to?

Really, Felix already knew what he'd do—he'd always been the curious sort. He slipped back inside and hid in the shadows of the empty stall that was next to Blackbird's. If the stranger intended mischief, he'd be in an excellent position to put paid to his plans and put all that training with his father to use. And if his intentions were more innocent, and it was just someone coming to take a break from his daily routine?

Well, the man in question *did* have marvellously broad shoulders, and Felix had more than fulfilled his own duties for the day. Perhaps, if the stranger was agreeable, he could offer him an afternoon's entertainment.

It couldn't hurt to ask.

## Chapter Four

Leopold slipped across the yard towards the stables. The homespun shirt that he'd filched from a pile in the laundry room was rough against skin that was more used to soft linen. He ignored the itch. It was a small price to pay for being able to move unseen through the castle.

He wasn't so foolish as to think he wouldn't be seen, but he'd done all he could to make himself unmemorable. He'd acquired a long leather coat from a hook on the back of the boot room door that trailed almost to the ground and hid most of his well-cut trousers—there was a limit to which garments belonging to strangers he was willing to wear, after all. He'd also worn his good riding boots in anticipation of being able to take Blackbird out, but once he'd hidden his distinctive dark hair with a battered hat that might have belonged to one of the gardeners, he was satisfied that a casual observer, at least, wouldn't mark him as anyone important.

After picking his way across the stretch of distance

between the laundry room and the stable, flattening himself against any available wall and checking that Mattias wasn't lying in wait for him as he sometimes did, he made it safely to the stables. He slipped inside and stood with his body pressed flat against the door, eyes adjusting to the dim interior. There was nobody in sight and he took a moment to inhale, the tension leaving him as his nostrils filled with the rich, familiar scents of fresh straw, horse sweat, and the undercurrent of dung. He sometimes wished he'd been born into a life like this rather than one of duty and expectation. But the thought was only ever fleeting and usually a result of petulance at being denied his own way. In reality, for all his grizzling, he was aware of his privileged position and knew that plenty of people would gladly trade places.

Besides, if he wasn't the king, he doubted he'd have a gorgeous girl like his Blackbird.

He approached the horse, admiring the state of her glossy black coat and well-brushed mane and tail. Whoever the new groom was, they knew what they were about. Leopold resolved to make time to meet them, if only so he could charm them into turning a blind eye when he wanted to sneak out like this. Mother Jones, his ridiculously named stable master, had standing instructions to send a boy to inform the chancellor, much to Leopold's chagrin.

Blackbird tossed her mane in recognition and Leopold petted her, running the flat of his palm along her cheek. "Hello there, pretty," he murmured. "Shall I take you for a ride?"

The horse nickered in agreement and blew out a great wet breath, turning her head and nuzzling hopefully against his hand. Leopold fed her the sugar lump he was hiding there and patted her cheek again before going to fetch his saddle. It was a bulky, heavy thing. Under normal circumstances he would have sent word and Blackbird would have been prepared for him by his groom, but Leopold had always prided himself on his fitness and it was no problem for him to lift the saddle from the rack where it was kept and carry it across the stables to Blackbird's stall. He was almost there when, from the darkness, a voice rang out.

"Tell me, have you a death wish?"

Leopold fumbled the saddle, almost dropping it, and whirled on his heel to find himself facing someone he'd never seen before. "What?"

A young man stood there, arms folded across his chest. He nodded at the saddle. "I only ask because that's the king's saddle, which makes me think you were about to steal the king's horse, and he won't take kindly to that."

Leopold took a moment to look his accuser over before replying. The young man was tall, lean but not lanky, and he had messy dark hair and expressive features that were marked by a determined crease between his brows. He was undeniably attractive beneath the frown.

This must be Blackbird's new groom, and he obviously had no idea who Leopold was. "Let me guess. You're the groom, and you're loyal to your king?" he said, secretly pleased at finding someone who was a devoted subject.

"What? Hells no. I don't give a damn about the king. But I've been warned that there's a stick jammed fair up the royal arse when it comes to his horse, and I'd like to keep my job past the first week. So if you could find a different horse to steal, or better still take none at all, I'd appreciate it."

Leopold raised an eyebrow. "And if I insist on taking this one?"

"Oh, then I'll definitely hunt you down and hurt you," the young man said without a trace of a smile. "It's my job."

Leopold let out a disbelieving snort, vaguely insulted that his impressive physique wasn't giving the young man so much as a moment's pause. "You think that *you* could hurt *me?*" He puffed out his chest. "I could bend you in half over that tack table and not even break a sweat doing it."

Leopold only realised what he'd said when a slow smile spread over the young man's face and his gaze travelled up and down Leopold's body in a manner that was both disconcerting and flattering and made Leopold's heart beat faster. "I'm sure you could, and with all that muscle of yours, I'd probably rather enjoy it. But bending me over the tables aside, I still can't let you take the king's horse, I'm afraid. Although you are rather handsome. Leave the horse and I might be persuaded to let you go if you win my favour." The groom's smile widened, and his eyes sparkled with mischief.

Leopold was torn between being offended by the young man's assertion that he had a stick up his arse and intrigued by his proposition—because it definitely *was* a proposition, judging by the way the groom appeared to be waiting for an answer. He decided to play along, the thrill of anonymity making him bold. "And how, exactly, would I win your favor?" he asked, lifting the saddle and hefting it over the rail of the stall while noting the way the young man's gaze followed his flexing muscles. He took a step so they were almost within touching distance, folded his arms over his chest in a way that displayed his build to best advantage, and waited.

The groom's tongue traced over his lower lip at the same time his gaze continued to roam over Leopold's body, his interest obvious. "I'm just saying that perhaps you could return that saddle, and instead of riding the horse, we could find another way to fill your afternoon and get your heart racing."

Oh, this was tremendous.

His new groom was *seducing* him. This was the most fun Leopold had had in ages, and if he played his cards right, it might just get better. He smirked and stepped up so close that they were almost toe to toe, placing himself firmly in the lad's space. It had been far too long since anyone had captured his interest like this fearless, forward little brat who was making his blood heat and want thrum through his veins in a way that he had sorely missed. "Are you suggesting a roll in the hay, sweetheart?" he purred, right into the lad's ear.

A deep flush rose on the boy's cheeks, the high colour only adding to his attractiveness, and Leopold desperately wanted to take him to bed, get his hands all over that lean frame, and make him blush for other, filthier reasons.

He had a moment of disappointment when the lad shook his head. "I would *never* suggest a roll in the hay." But then the boy smirked and said, "Everyone knows hay's far too scratchy. But there's a decent bed in my cottage if you're interested."

"Oh, I'm interested if you are," Leopold breathed out, sliding a hand around to the small of the lad's back.

The groom's breathing hitched and his eyes widened before he leaned in and kissed Leopold without warning. Leopold, heady with excitement and ever-growing arousal, kissed him right back. He found himself swept up in the way the young man's mouth moved against his expertly, their tongues brushing, and the warmth of the lad's hand where it came to rest on the nape of his neck and settled there. They kissed until Leopold was breathless, and when the groom pulled back, he was grinning, eyes bright and lips ruby red and plump.

Leopold wanted nothing more than to ruin him.

He gripped the lad's hips, pulling him closer and murmuring, "Tell me, do you have a name? I need to know what to call the man who's seducing me, surely?"

"Felix," The boy breathed out. "It's Felix."

"Felix." Leopold rolled the name on his tongue like a rich port, tasting it.

"And you?" Felix asked, raising an eyebrow. Leopold's mind blanked for a second. "Or do horse thieves not have names?" Felix's mouth quirked upward.

"I—uh—Leopold," he stammered. It had been so long since anyone had asked him who he was, it honestly didn't occur to him to give anything but his real name.

"Oh, so because you share a name with the king, you thought you could share his mount as well?" Felix's grin widened.

"My father was a staunch royalist," Leopold said. It wasn't a lie.

He slid his hands around from Felix's hips, letting

them roam up and down his back, exploring all that lean muscle and promise. When he squeezed ever so gently at that perfect peach of an arse, Felix let out a tiny whimper before surging forward and pressing Leopold back against the door of Blackbird's stall. He plastered their bodies together and kissed him again, hungry and demanding, and Leopold's cock stirred and thickened in his trousers.

Felix slid a hand between them and rubbed at the growing bulge there. "It seems someone's agreeable to an afternoon delight."

Leopold's knees threatened to buckle as something like lightning coursed through him at the intimate touch—which was patently ridiculous, he was the *king* for heaven's sake—but somehow Felix had managed to bewitch him. He couldn't say he minded. It had been a long time since he'd been this attracted to another man.

"Won't you get in trouble for deserting your post?" he asked, even as he rocked against Felix's hand. "After all, you're supposed to be guarding the royal mount."

Felix's answering grin was a mischievous thing that Leopold wanted to lick out of his mouth. "Technically, I'm detaining a potential thief. And I've had no word that the king will ride today, so we shouldn't be disturbed. So, what do you say?"

"Hmmm." Leopold wrapped his arms around Felix's neck and leaned in for another longer kiss. "Yes," he said once they parted. "You've convinced me to leave the horse alone and take a different sort of ride."

Felix let out a warm, rich laugh, then cupped Leopold's erection once again and caressed him through the cloth, the sensation so delicious that Leopold whimpered. Felix pulled back and took his hand away and Leopold was at once bereft, but it turned out that Felix had only moved so that he could steer them into the empty stall and give them more privacy.

Once there, he cupped Leopold's face in his hands and kissed him, soft and delicate, and the confidence of his movements gave the impression that Felix knew exactly what he was doing and would likely prove an excellent cocksman. Leopold certainly hoped so, since it had been far too long since his last assignation. He slid his hands down Felix's back and slipped one hand under the hem of his shirt and back up, skating his fingertips over Felix's ribs and soaking up the feel of bare skin under his touch. Felix moaned against his mouth and ground forward, his cock a hard line as he rocked against the bulge in Leopold's trousers and pulled the collar of his shirt aside, peppering little kisses along his collarbone.

Leopold tilted his head to the side to allow better access, rutting forward against Felix's cock and savouring the frisson of arousal that ran through him. "Can I fuck you, Felix?" he murmured.

"Please, Leo." Felix's breath was warm against the damp skin where the ghost of his kisses lived.

"Oh, it's *Leo* now, is it? That seems awfully familiar." Leopold was aware how ridiculous he sounded given what they were currently doing, but he was having *fun*. He hadn't met anyone so delightfully disrespectful in a long time, and he intended to make the most of it.

"Well, I can't exactly call you Leopold, can I?" Felix said, pulling back and running a hand through his hair. "Leopold is the *king*, whereas Leo is a very sexy horse thief I met in the stables. If you insist on me calling you Leopold, I'm afraid I'll have to call the whole thing off." He took another step back and stood in an insouciant slouch, one hand perched on his hip with an eyebrow raised in silent challenge.

*Delightful.*

"I've always felt Leo had a nice ring to it," Leopold said, right before he grabbed Felix by his shirtfront and swung him around so that his back hit the wall of the stall hard enough that the timbers shook. Felix sucked in a sharp breath and his eyes darkened. He reached a hand out and fumbled with Leo's belt, and Leo's cock throbbed in anticipation of Felix's touch. Behind them, the horse whinnied loudly and hooves clattered as Blackbird moved about, and then her head came into view and she nuzzled at the side of Felix's head. He let go of Leo's belt and, laughing, shoved at her head.

Leo huffed in frustration. "Not now, Blackbird."

Felix froze against him at the same moment Leopold realised his mistake.

"What did you call her?" Felix stepped to one side so he was out of Leopold's reach and tilted his head, his eyes flicking up and down as if seeing him for the first time before settling on the expensive leather riding boots that Leopold was wearing. "Those aren't the boots of a scoundrel or a thief. They're top quality."

"Yes, they are."

"And your trousers are far too fine for a commoner." Felix's eyes widened, and Leo could see the moment the truth dawned on him. "You're—you're not stealing this horse, are you?"

"No, I'm not," Leopold agreed with a sigh.

Felix made a high-pitched noise in his throat and continued to back away, a tremor in his voice as he pointed at Blackbird. "This is—is this *your* horse? Are you—are you *him*?"

"The king with the stick up his arse?" Leopold sighed again, inexplicably disappointed. "That would be me, yes."

He'd been having *fun,* and now that Felix knew who he was, he was doubtless going to turn into just another apologetic forelock-tugging lackey, and Leo wouldn't get to spend the afternoon naked with this delightfully pretty lad after all.

Instead of bowing and scraping, though, Felix took a couple of rapid breaths and, apparently having gathered his wits, turned an accusing finger on Leo. "You set me up! You let me insult you and proposition you, and now I'm going to get sacked for it, aren't I? And what are you even doing here? I was specifically told that if you wanted to ride, I'd get plenty of warning, and instead you come skulking down here dressed in God knows what—" He broke off mid-sentence and took a step closer, eyes narrowed. "Did you *steal* that coat?" Leopold felt warm breath against his cheek as Felix leaned in and examined the coat more closely. "You did! That's my father's coat! He's captain of the guard, not that you'd care. Anyway, you can't just go around taking people's clothes for your own entertainment. What's he meant to wear home at the end of his shift?"

Leo's eyebrows rose. The only one who dared to speak to him like that was Mattias, and he probably should have been offended, but instead he found himself intrigued, if only by the sheer size of the balls on his new groom.

"Your father is captain of the guard?" he asked, to give himself time to regroup.

Felix nodded, jerky and suspicious. "So?"

"Janus is a good man."

"Yeah, he is." Felix sighed and fixed his gaze on the ground. "So, I guess you're going to relieve me of my position now. *Your Majesty*," he added belatedly, and it sounded suspiciously like *Fuck you*.

Leo couldn't help but smirk. Perhaps all wasn't lost if the boy still had some spark left in his belly. "Let's see. So far, you've accused me of being a horse thief, implied that you'd only release me if I slept with you, and then, when you found out who I really am, yelled at me for *borrowing* a coat and shirt from the laundry. I really *should* dismiss you."

Felix's head snapped up at that. "You never said you *weren't* stealing the horse," he argued hotly, "so technically, I *was* doing my job."

"And the part where you tried to seduce me?" Leo asked, enjoying himself enormously now that he was back in control.

Felix's mouth opened and closed again, and then he shrugged as if he knew that what he said wouldn't matter. "I thought you were my type, and I wanted to get you into bed. Looks like that won't be happening now either."

Leo couldn't help the laugh that came bubbling up out of him. Such refreshing honesty was rare, and he found himself wanting more of it—more of *Felix*. And having it confirmed that the attraction went both ways was just the icing on the cake as far as he was concerned.

He rested a hand on Felix's shoulder, gratified when Felix didn't flinch away but instead gave an uncertain smile. "I suppose that you did only threaten to harm me to protect Blackbird, even if she is my own horse," Leo said, mind ticking over, "which means you've proven yourself loyal. So no, I'm not going to dismiss you." He was distracted for a moment by the way Felix's face lit up with a hopeful expression and by the curve of his lush, Cupid's bow mouth, but he managed to drag his gaze away and get back to the matter at hand. "I can't help but feel there's a better place for you than the stables, though. Given who your father is, I'm assuming you've been trained in the defensive arts?"

Felix nodded rapidly. "Weapons and hand to hand both."

"So why haven't you joined the guard? Are you such a terrible soldier?" Felix ending up in the stables just didn't make sense otherwise.

Felix bristled. "I'm good! But I didn't want to work for my father. In the guard I'd be under his eye all day, and I wanted—" He swallowed. "I wanted to be able to have a roll in the hay without my dad knowing about it, okay? And I'm good with horses, so Mattias—I mean, Chancellor Allingdon—arranged for me to train in Fortescue. I worked there until he invited me back to take the position in the stables."

"So that's why I haven't seen you before," Leo mused. "You've been away."

Felix nodded. "Six years, sire."

Leo hummed in response, mind whirring with possibilities. Felix, far from crumbling under royal disapproval, had shown himself to possess a spine of steel, which made him even more attractive, and Leo found himself intrigued. He still wanted to bed him, of course, but he also wanted to get to know him better.

If Felix was telling the truth about his skill with a weapon, he might actually be the solution to several problems at once, assuming he was willing, of course. Well, there was only one way to find out.

"Follow me," Leo said and turned on his heel and marched back to the castle. He didn't bother to check and see if Felix had followed him, but smiled when he heard footsteps behind him hurrying to catch up.

He did so love a young man who could take direction.

## Chapter Five

Felix followed the king—*the king!*—across the courtyard, silently thanking the gods that instead of being dismissed on the spot like he'd expected, he was being summoned to the castle. He wasn't sure why, but he took some reassurance from the fact that Leopold didn't seem angry about Felix berating him. In fact, Felix would say he'd seemed more amused than anything. That could only be a good thing, in Felix's book.

Leo's boots were loud against the worn cobblestones as he strode towards the castle, and he walked with a confidence that was in direct contrast to the way he'd slipped silently towards the stables when Felix had pegged him for a thief. Felix caught up soon enough but stayed back, some long-forgotten edict of royal etiquette that had been drummed into him as a child rising up and keeping him one step back and to the right. They cut across the courtyard and around the back, along the narrow alleyway that led to the entrance to the laundry area and boot room, and the king ushered Felix inside.

The king discarded his borrowed coat and hat, hanging them on one of the bent nails that had been fashioned into hooks, and the familiarity with which he moved around the room made Felix suspect that this wasn't the first time Leopold had slipped out of the castle unguarded. In all honesty, Felix couldn't really blame him. He couldn't imagine what it would be like to be so important that every move was scrutinised, or to never have anyone speak their mind frankly in case it earned them a royal reprimand. It must be exhausting. Perhaps that was why the king was more entertained than irate at Felix's irreverent attitude.

Whatever the case, Felix was grateful if it meant he got to keep his job.

Leopold eased his borrowed shirt off over his head and Felix couldn't help the sound of admiration that escaped him. He'd known the king was in good shape, but he hadn't expected so much muscle, or for the smooth planes of Leo's back to ripple *quite* so enticingly.

Leopold turned and raised one eyebrow at him, and Felix half expected to be chastised for gazing upon the royal person, but instead a slow smile crept across the king's features. Leo straightened his spine and placed his hands on his hips, pulling his shoulders back to emphasise the breadth of his chest in what had to be a deliberate show.

Felix licked his lips, unable to look away from the broad expanse of muscle and the lightly tanned skin complete with tight brown nipples and a light smattering of dark chest hair that became a tempting trail that disappeared into the king's trousers.

"See something you like, lovely?" Leo asked.

Felix felt his face heat.

Leo smirked. "Don't tell me you're suddenly shy? You were going to fuck me in your cottage not ten minutes ago. I was quite looking forward to it."

*Oh?*

A part of Felix—his dick, probably—was thrilled to note that fucking *wasn't* off the table after all. But the rest of him possessed at least a modicum of self-preservation. "That was before I knew you were the king!" he protested. He paused as his brain caught up. "Wait, weren't you going to fuck me?"

"Details," Leo said, his smile widening. He retrieved a fine linen shirt from another hook and slipped it over his head. Even untucked, the cut and quality of the garment bestowed an air of authority, and Felix wondered how he could ever have mistaken Leo for a common thief.

In fact, now that he was looking for it, Felix could see traces of the young prince he'd insulted when he was just a boy. Leo still had the same dark hair, high cheekbones, sculpted jawline, and aquiline nose, but now those features were imbued with the traces of character that had been gained with time, and rather than detracting from his looks, they elevated Leo into true handsomeness.

The king's blue eyes seemed to pierce Felix's very soul as he stalked over to where he was still lingering near the door. He placed one hand on Felix's hip and the other under his chin, tilting it up so Felix couldn't have looked away even if he'd wanted to.

Not that he *did* want to.

The king leaned in close and murmured against the

shell of Felix's ear. "We can discuss the finer points of the arrangement later, but I would still very much like to take you to bed, Felix."

He pressed a delicate kiss to Felix's mouth, a tiny little thing that was the barest brush of lips against his. It was hardly anything, but it was enough to have Felix melting into the king's touch. He didn't resist when Leo leaned forward and kissed him again, instead closing his eyes and letting himself get lost in the plushness of Leo's mouth and the heat of his body, and resting his hands on Leo's shoulders. Leo moved closer, bracketing him against the wall and placing both hands on Felix's hips as if he were afraid Felix might try and run.

*Not likely.*

Felix could have stayed here all day just kissing, running his hands down Leo's broad back and feeling the play of muscle under the linen shirt. He was very much aware, though, that this was the *king* he was kissing and that the laundry room was possibly the worst place in the castle to conduct anything that required an ounce of privacy, on account of almost every servant who worked in the kitchen or the yards passing through at some stage of the day.

His instincts were proven correct when, just as he ended the kiss and slipped his hands from around the king, he heard Mother calling out, "Flick? Are you in—"

Leo took a step back and dropped his hands to his sides right before Mother Jones appeared in the doorway.

He stopped short, glancing between them, and cleared his throat. "Oh. Apologies, Your Majesty. I was just looking for Felix but I see he's, ah, busy."

Felix ducked his head, feigning interest in the dust patterns on the stone floor.

"Mr. Jones," Leo said pleasantly, like he hadn't just had his tongue inside Felix's mouth. "I was just introducing myself to my new groom."

"Right." Mother nodded, not quite managing to hide his smile before turning on his heel and departing. He was gone before the flush of heat at almost being caught had left Felix's cheeks.

When he lifted his head, Leo was looking at him with open curiosity. "He called you Flick," he said. "Why do I know that name?" Leo's brow furrowed in concentration in a way that reminded Felix of a small child first learning to trace their letters.

Felix bit his lip. "We've met before. When I was younger."

It took a moment, but then Leo's eyes widened. "You're the brat who insulted me!"

Felix nodded, his heart sinking, and waited for the inevitable outrage followed by his dismissal. So much for his new position.

But Leo didn't seem upset by his revelation. In fact, his face broke into a wide smile, and he threw his head back and *laughed*. "What was it you called me? A self-important twat?"

"Actually, I called you a stuck-up little tit. But in my defence, I didn't know you were the prince."

Leo snorted in a manner most unbecoming to a monarch. "So, you were just rude to everybody as a child, I take it."

Felix couldn't help himself. "Possibly. But now that I

know who you are, I'll be sure to show proper deference and not call you names...unless you'd like that."

Leo's eyebrows rose in surprise and Felix wondered if he'd overstepped, but then a hungry smile crept over Leo's face and he leant in close again and whispered, "Well, I will admit I don't mind hearing the occasional *sire.*"

Felix's heart pounded in his chest and he could feel warmth suffusing his cheeks.

"Oh, you do blush so prettily, sweetheart," Leo crooned. "I can't wait to see how far down it goes." He held out a hand. "Come up to my rooms? We won't be disturbed there."

Felix took his hand and was rewarded with a dazzling smile as Leo led the way through the kitchens, weaving his way among the controlled chaos with easy confidence and being ignored by the staff in a way that suggested this was a common occurrence. He guided Felix up one, then another set of dim, dusty stairs that a king was probably never meant to know about, let alone traverse. As if sensing the question, Leo said, "Mattias and I explored every inch of the castle when he first came to live here. I know every way in and out there is. He was meant to keep me out of mischief, but I'm not sure if he succeeded entirely."

"And you and he never..." Felix let the question linger.

"Never. We're more like brothers. Mattias will defend me to the death, but also tell me if I'm being an arse—which he does far more often than I care to admit. He's my necessary but inconvenient voice of reason."

"And what would your voice of reason say if he found you sneaking a servant into your room in the middle of the day?"

Leo turned a corner and ducked the cobwebs hanging there with the ease of long practice before he answered. "He'd probably tell me to lock the door because he doesn't want to walk in on that twice in one lifetime."

Felix let out a bark of laughter. Leo was turning out to be very different to how Felix had imagined a king. Rather than an officious stuffed shirt, here was a man who was not only clever and handsome, but also had no hesitation in admitting his attraction to Felix.

*And don't forget that comment about being called sire,* his brain reminded him helpfully. *He might even like the same things you do.*

They reached a narrow corridor at the top of the staircase, and Leo paused long enough to drag Felix close and kiss him, his tongue pressing against the seam of Felix's lips, seeking admission. Felix closed his eyes, losing himself to Leo's tongue filling the spaces in his mouth and kissing back with vigour. Leo pulled back and ran his hands over the curve of Felix's arse. "You really are a delight," he murmured, "and I can't wait to see you in my bed."

"And yet here we are, kissing in a secret passage because *you* wanted to stop," Felix pointed out, grinning.

"You make a fair point." Leo placed his hands on Felix's hips and turned him so he was facing the door at the end of the passageway. "Don't dawdle, sweetheart."

He followed the words up with a light slap to Felix's backside. It barely stung, but it still had Felix gasping in both shock and arousal as he stumbled forward. Maybe Leo really *did* like to play the same games Felix did. The thought had his cock throbbing, and he covered the length of the passageway in half a dozen long strides. Leo followed on, pressing himself against Felix's back and wrapping an arm around his chest before he opened the door.

It led into yet another corridor, but this one gave the impression of frequent and public use, so Felix guessed they were back in the castle proper. It was only a short walk till they reached a set of double doors which opened to reveal the royal quarters. Leo herded him inside and Felix went willingly.

Once in, Leo locked the door before leaning back against it and letting out a satisfied sigh. "Here we are. Do you like it?"

Felix stepped forward and took in the room before him. The stone walls were decorated with thick tapestries, the intricate stitching depicting various hunting scenes, and there was a low-burning fire with two well-worn chairs next to it as well as a washstand and a desk in opposite corners of the room. The floor was covered with a rug that was probably worth more than Felix earned in a year, but he only gave it a passing glance. Most of his attention was taken up by the bed—a great broad thing, a four-poster with ornate patterning carved into the posts and covered in a thick quilt of deepest blue. It sported a pile of thick feather pillows, and Felix could only imagine what it would feel like to be nestled naked amongst the linens next to another warm body.

*Leo's* body, specifically.

He cleared his throat. "The bed looks much more comfortable than the one in my cottage."

Leo's eyes lit up and he stepped forward, draping his arms around Felix's neck to pull him in close and resting his head in the curve of his throat. "Mmmm. Probably. Shall we test it out and see?"

"Please." Felix, thrilled at Leo's closeness, trailed his fingertips down the nape of Leo's muscled neck and was rewarded with a shudder and a soft moan. Emboldened, Felix dragged his fingers down the length of Leo's spine and squeezed his arse lightly, and this time he was the one to pull Leo towards him so that their cocks rubbed together. The sensation was almost overwhelming, even through the cloth of his trousers.

Leo let out a shuddery breath. "You should know it's cruel to tease, sweetheart."

"Surely it's only teasing if I intend to stop," Felix said quietly, his heart hammering in his chest at the endearment. He stepped backward towards the bed, tugging Leo along with him. Their bodies rubbed together in a constant tease that had his cock straining at the laces. By the time they'd made it as far as the rug, Felix didn't want to wait any longer to see if the royal cock was as impressive as the bulge in Leo's trousers promised. He dropped to his knees, reaching out to steady himself against Leo's thick thighs. "Can I taste you?"

Leo froze, letting out a groan.

Felix tilted his head back to seek the king's permission and found Leo watching him, eyes dark and glittering, his mouth hanging open. Felix undid the fastenings on Leo's trousers, fumbling in his haste, and shoved his clothing halfway down his thighs before wrapping a hand around his cock, which was every bit as impressive as Felix had hoped. A decent length, it also boasted a nice thick girth, and Felix couldn't wait to feel the weight of it on his tongue. It was flushed a rosy pink and damp at the head, straining upward as if it had a mind of its own—and perhaps it did.

Lord knew, Felix's own cock had done plenty of thinking for him in the past.

Felix spread his knees wider so that he was at the right height to do this comfortably, then leaned in and swiped his tongue across the tip in a kitten lick to catch the droplet of liquid there. The taste of salt and spend burst across his tongue, as intoxicating as always. Felix took the head of Leo's cock in his mouth, teasing and licking, swirling his tongue in a way that made Leo's breath hitch. He'd always loved this, being able to make someone fall apart with just his mouth, and the knowledge that this was the *king*, the ruler of the entire kingdom, made the experience all the more satisfying. His own erection throbbed, impatient, and Felix pressed down on the front of his trousers with one palm.

"Gods, your *mouth*," Leo gasped out, tangling his fingers in the strands of Felix's hair and tugging. The sting was unexpected but no less sweet for that, and Felix rewarded the movement by taking more of Leo's length into his mouth and sliding up and down, letting his tongue dance along the shaft as he did so.

Leo made a sound like he'd been punched and rolled his hips, matching Felix's rhythm. The hands in his hair tightened and pre-cum spurted across Felix's tongue.

Felix hummed, his senses filled with the taste and feel of Leo. It was a heady, addictive mix. He bobbed his head, sucking and licking, soaking up the hungry, desperate noises Leo was making as his hips rocked forward with more purpose. It wasn't long until, after a particularly urgent thrust, Leo let out a deep, guttural groan and pulled Felix's head forward with both hands, holding him in place as he spilled down Felix's throat. Felix swallowed every drop.

Leo's grip loosened and he ran his fingers through Felix's tousled hair. Felix let Leo's softening cock slip from his mouth, turning his head so he was resting his cheek against Leo's thigh, the thick muscle solid and comforting as he drew in several deep breaths. The tang of Leo's spend was fresh in his mouth and he licked his lips, chasing more of the taste.

Leo gave a guiding pull on his locks, causing him to tilt his head back, and placed a hand in the middle of his chest, shoving gently at him until Felix found himself sprawled on his back on the rug. Leo raised an eyebrow and dropped to his knees between Felix's legs, and before Felix could ask what he was doing, Leo had undone Felix's trousers, licked his palm, and wrapped his now-damp hand around Felix's straining cock. He started to jerk Felix off with short, urgent movements that were just this side of too rough and absolutely perfect. Felix wanted it to last forever but his treacherous body had other ideas, and it took less than a minute before heat raced through Felix's veins and gathered in his groin, his cock throbbing like a second heartbeat. Leo smirked and gave a clever twist of his wrist on the upstroke, and Felix's spine arched like a longbow as he panted and came in hot spurts over Leo's hand.

Felix shivered and gasped while Leo worked him through it in slow, steady movements until he couldn't take it anymore and batted Leo's hand away, mumbling, "S'too much."

Felix's body tingled with warmth and satisfaction. He sprawled on the rug, boneless and content, and closed his eyes. He wasn't sure how long he lay there for, but he might have dozed off. It was only when he felt a hand carding through his hair that he opened his eyes again.

Leo was gazing down at him like…well. Like a king about to bestow a benediction on his subject.

Felix waited for him to say something—anything—and the silence stretched long enough that he was just beginning to worry he'd fallen asleep for too long and breached some mysterious royal protocol when Leo finally spoke. "Come and work for me."

Felix struggled into a sitting position. "I already work for you."

Leo let out a soft sigh. "You work for the castle. I want you to work for *me*. As part of my personal retinue. I have the perfect position for you."

His smile was wicked as he said it, and something twisted in Felix's gut as what the king was suggesting made itself clear.

Leo wanted him as his *whore*.

He felt a tiny flicker of annoyance, and before he knew it, that flicker had become a blaze. He gestured angrily, his mouth running away with him. "I trained for *four years* to be a groom, and then it was another two years of late nights and early mornings and mucking out stalls, learning my trade and gaining a skill to do a job that I love. And now that you've decided you'd like me as a bedmate, I'm meant to throw it all away to be your fucking *pet,* is that it?"

Leo's mouth dropped open and his brow furrowed. "No? Why would you think that?"

Felix scrambled to his feet and tucked his still-damp cock into his trousers in an effort to retain at least a shred of dignity, then raised an eyebrow in a mirror image of the look his father gave to particularly stupid recruits. "You tell me to follow you without a word of explanation, take me to the royal bedroom, and after you've sampled the wares, you tell me you want me to work for you *personally*. What am I meant to think?"

Leo took a deep breath and exhaled slowly before he stood, rubbing a hand down the side of his face and shaking his head. "You misunderstand me, Felix. I find you an attractive, intelligent, and frankly fuckable young man who isn't afraid to tell me what he thinks—which, believe me, is a rarity in my world—and for those reasons alone, I want you in my bed. But that's not the position I'd like to offer you."

Felix frowned in confusion, even as his insides churned in a mix of hope and a lingering trace of hurt that Leo thought so little of him. He desperately wanted to be wrong, because he'd thought he liked Leo, and he *did* want to grace his bed—but not at the cost of everything he'd worked for. "So, the new position isn't on my knees?"

Leo's mouth twisted with the hint of a suppressed smile. "I'd like you to be my *bodyguard,* Felix. In addition to your position as my groom, of course."

*Oh.*

The hope in Felix's belly flared. "What, *exactly,* would that entail?"

"You'd accompany me when I take Blackbird out and

keep me safe. It would mean I could ride most days while freeing the guards or Mattias from having to trail along behind me when I want to leave the castle. Believe me, he'll be thrilled with the idea."

Felix allowed himself to relax, his shoulders creeping down from where he'd pulled them up around his ears. "So the sex wouldn't be part of my employment? That's just because we want to?"

"Absolutely," Leo assured him, eyes gleaming—with amusement or anticipation, Felix couldn't quite tell. "It would have no bearing on your other duties."

Felix thought about it. It sounded like an ideal arrangement, but part of him wanted to make Leo squirm before he agreed to anything. "And what if I don't *want* to be your bodyguard?"

Leo rolled his eyes and stood, pulling Felix close and kissing him. Felix responded eagerly, and by the time Leo pulled back they were both grinning. Felix let out a soft laugh, happiness bubbling up in his chest at the thought that maybe he could have this. "If you're going to kiss me like that every time I disagree with you, I might never shut up."

"Oh, I have other methods for taking care of mouthy brats," Leo said. Then his mouth snapped shut and his cheeks flushed dark red, and Felix got the feeling the king hadn't meant to say that out loud. He wasn't going to let something like that go unremarked, though, not if it meant what he *hoped* it meant.

"Oh?" He leaned in close and whispered, "Would those methods involve your hand, my bare arse, and being put across your lap?" He tried to hide the excitement in his voice, but he wasn't quite sure he managed it.

Leo's eyes widened before he let out a low, filthy chuckle, and the smile he gave promised nothing but trouble of the most enjoyable kind. "I should warn you, Felix, I like nothing better than a good, obedient lad who does as he's told—unless it's a naughty boy who knows how to take a spanking."

Despite having just come, Felix's cock twitched.

"Tell me. Tell me what you'd do," he demanded, hardly able to believe his good fortune.

Leo's voice was barely a breath in Felix's ear. "I promise, sweetheart, that if you misbehave, I won't hesitate to put you over my knee and spank you till your arse is pink and tender. And if you're a very good boy, I'll fuck you afterwards and make you feel it." Felix couldn't hold back a groan. Leo tipped Felix's chin up with a fingertip, holding his gaze. "I need a yes or a no, sweetheart."

"Y-yes," Felix stammered out before Leo could change his mind.

Leo's eyes were dark as he cupped Felix's face with one hand. "So you'd like that, being my boy?"

Felix didn't reply, instead tangling his hands in Leo's hair and pulling him in and kissing him, hot and desperate. "I'd like that a lot," he breathed out once they'd parted, lips still tingling and stomach swooping with anticipation.

"And the position as my bodyguard?"

Felix rolled his eyes. "Yes, fine. But I want my own horse," he added, feeling bold. "I want Shadow."

Leo's face lit up with a pleased smile. "Right now, you can have anything you want."

Felix grinned back. "In that case? I want you to take me to bed and show me if you're any good."

The words had barely left his mouth when he found himself swept up in strong arms and carried across the bedroom.

Leo dropped him on the mattress. "That," he said, his voice thick with want, "would be my absolute pleasure."

## Chapter Six

Leo took in the sight of a grinning Felix sprawled across his bed and felt his own mouth curve into a smile. If he was lucky, he might be able to keep Felix for the rest of the afternoon, perhaps even into the evening. There were no pressing matters of state, no meetings, nothing urgent that he needed to attend to at all. The only thing that demanded his attention right now was getting Felix out of his clothes and possibly over his lap.

First, though, he needed to ensure they weren't disturbed. To that end he said, "Wait here. I'll be right back," then fastened his trousers and strode out of the room. He hurried along the corridor and down two sets of stairs, stopping outside Mattias's offices. He nodded at the guard standing there. "Is he in?"

"Yes, Your Majesty."

Leo didn't bother to ask if Mattias was *free*—he was the king, and as such his needs took precedence over anything else Mattias was doing. He poked his head in the door and Mattias looked up and smiled. "Finished with the correspondence?"

"That's not why I'm here," Leo said, hedging, having forgotten the stack of paperwork he was meant to be dealing with. "I just wanted to tell you I'm not to be disturbed until morning unless it's life or death, except to deliver two trays for supper."

Mattias stood, giving Leo a suspicious look. "*Two* trays?"

Leo grinned. "Let's just say that since you wouldn't allow me to go riding without a guard, I've arranged alternative entertainment."

"But you were meant to be in your office working. How have you managed—" Mattias let out a heavy sigh. "Never mind. Forget that I asked."

"That's probably for the best," Leo agreed, and ducked out of the room before Mattias decided to ask awkward questions after all.

He scampered back up the stairs, anticipation fizzing under his skin. When he got back to his chambers, he had to stop for a second and stare. While he'd been gone, Felix had stripped naked and was now sprawled cross his bed, all long, lean-muscled limbs and milky flesh, and his cock, pink and enticing, was draped in a most beguiling manner against his thigh. He looked mouth-watering.

He looked like he *belonged*.

Felix's eyes were bright with anticipation, and he ran his tongue over his bottom lip while looking Leo up and down. "So tell me, were you planning to get your arse out of those trousers anytime soon? Because I'm a busy man. I have horses to tend, stable boys to terrorise, and a royal body to guard. I can't just lie about in bed all day while you stand there gawping." He gave a mischievous grin.

"*So* disrespectful." Leo sat on the edge of the bed and dragged his boots off, then stood and removed the rest of his clothing. Felix's eyes darkened and his breathing sped up at the sight of Leo's naked form, and Leo felt a thrum of satisfaction at the want written all over his face. Leo reached out a hand and skated his fingertips down Felix's side before stroking the curve of his hip and tracing a hand across his belly. Felix's skin was soft and smooth, and it would colour so prettily under a firm hand. "I did warn you what I do with mouthy brats, didn't I?"

"Oh, was that a warning? I thought it was a promise." Felix grinned, rolling over onto his stomach and propping himself on his elbows so that his deliciously pert arse was on display. "Yet here I am, unrepentant and unspanked."

"The nerve of you! It's almost like you *want* me to put you over my lap," Leo said, wondering all the while how he'd gotten so lucky.

"Obviously." Felix's grin widened.

There was nothing Leo would have liked more than to bend Felix over the side of the bed right then and indulge his fantasies of seeing that peach-perfect arse tinged pink. But the more sensible part of himself, the part that oversaw an entire kingdom and engaged in diplomacy and negotiation on a daily basis, was aware that sometimes people only *thought* they knew what they wanted and were unprepared for the reality of it. He needed to be sure that Felix was serious about what he was asking for.

He cupped Felix's jaw in one hand and caught his gaze. "Are you sure? Is this *really* something you enjoy?" He was desperate for the answer to be yes, and he found himself holding his breath as he waited.

Felix huffed impatiently. "Well, I wouldn't have suggested it otherwise, would I? Trust me, I *enjoy* these kinds of games." He lifted one eyebrow and wiggled his arse in blatant invitation, one that Leo had no intention of refusing now that he was assured of Felix's enthusiasm.

Leo reached across and slapped Felix's arse cheek, which earned him a yelp followed by a delighted laugh. Leo found himself unable to look away from the pink handprint that bloomed against the pale skin, flesh jiggling with the impact of the blow.

Felix rolled to face him, eyes wide. "Shall I climb on your lap?"

"Yes," Leo said, voice rough with want. "Over my knee, and you get ten for your cheek."

"I think you'll find I have two cheeks. Do I get ten for each?" Felix asked as he squirmed across the bed and draped himself over Leo's lap—and oh, he'd *obviously* done this before if the way he positioned himself in a perfect arch, with fingers and toes touching the ground, was anything to go by.

"You'll get what I give you, brat," Leo said, trying to sound stern and failing. He eased Felix forward a bare half inch so his cock slotted more comfortably into the gap of Leo's thighs and braced a forearm over the small of Felix's back, rubbing over the tantalising globes of flesh with an open palm and indulging in the sheer pleasure of having his fingertips drag over such delightfully soft skin.

He gave a series of gentle taps to warm the skin, and when he deemed Felix ready, he delivered a single sharp slap, the act making his blood heat and his palm tingle. "All right?" he asked quietly and waited until Felix nodded before delivering three more in quick succession. He alternated between left and right, and as he'd suspected, Felix's arse coloured up beautifully under his touch.

Felix let out a shaky moan and Leo felt a wave of desire roll over him. He raised his hand and connected with the soft flesh twice more. He stopped for a moment to smooth his palm over the delightfully pink globes, breathing heavily. It had been too long since he'd indulged himself like this. He wasn't the only one affected. He could feel Felix's erection pressing against his thigh, and he was reassured that the boy was enjoying this as much as he was.

He aimed his next blows across the crease at the top of Felix's thighs and added a touch more force, which earned him a high-pitched squeal.

Leo stilled his hand. "Too much?"

Felix shook his head, squirming in his hold. "No, sire! It's—more, *please?*" His voice quavered, but Leo had done this enough times to recognise that it was shaking with need, not distress.

A thrill ran through Leo at the desperation in the boy's voice, his own arousal spiking as Felix rutted against his leg. "Oh, so you've found your manners? Excellent. Let's be sure the lesson sticks, shall we?"

And with that, he peppered the rosy pink skin of Felix's backside with a rapid series of blows, his blood thundering in his ears and his cock throbbing in time with his heartbeat. Felix writhed and whimpered under him, hips rocking faster, until Leo stopped holding back and delivered a final series of ringing slaps to the boy's arse.

"Hah!" Felix cried out, bucking against Leo's hold, and wetness and warmth pulsed against the bare skin of Leo's thighs as his impossible, perfect boy spilled his seed.

Felix slumped across Leo's lap, his body a solid, boneless weight as he let out a series of shuddery breaths. His arse was now a glorious deep shade of pink, and Leo could feel the warmth radiating from the skin when he ran a careful hand over it.

Felix let out a breathy sigh. "You're good at that," he slurred, struggling to climb out of Leo's lap.

Leo caught him around the waist and helped him roll onto the bed where he lay facedown and spread-eagled, his face as flushed as his arse and wearing a wide, sloppy grin. He patted the bed in invitation and Leo didn't hesitate, placing a hand on Felix's hip and rolling him to the side before curling up behind him.

It meant his cock came in contact with the heat of Felix's arse, but Felix didn't pull away from the touch. Instead, he let out a soft groan and pulled his top leg forward. Then he reached back with a clumsy hand and scooped some of the mess from Leo's skin and spread the handful of his own spend between his thighs. The sight was unbearably erotic, and Leo almost came from the sight of it—and it only got better when Felix pressed his legs together, wrapped his hand around Leo's erection, and guided it into the warm, wet cavern he'd created. Leo grunted in shock when Felix deliberately tensed around him, and he couldn't have stopped himself rutting forward if he'd tried. It took barely a dozen thrusts before his arousal overtook him. Heat and lightning raced down his spine and gathered in his belly as he pulled Felix close and buried his face in the curve of his neck, panting out his release as he spilled into the tight space.

Felix gave a soft, teasing laugh. "Ask me again if I enjoy getting spanked."

"Mmm." It was the best Leo could manage, overwhelmed not only by two orgasms, but also the turn the day had taken. He'd started out with back-to-back meetings and an expectation that he'd be buried in paperwork for the afternoon, but somehow he'd ended up buried in the arms of a lover instead.

In his opinion, this was far preferable.

Felix's skin was warm against his, and he nuzzled in closer as his breathing slowed and he waited for the pleasant fog brought on by his release to lift from his mind. Felix squirmed in his arms until they were face-to-face, reaching out to run a hand through Leo's dishevelled hair.

"I really did like it," he said, quietly earnest, "and I like *you*."

"I like you too, darling," Leo said, throwing an arm over Felix's shoulders and leaning in to press a kiss to his cheek. "So, did I meet your standards? Are you agreeable to this becoming a regular arrangement?"

Felix hesitated. "Won't you get into trouble with Mattias for bedding the staff?"

Leo snorted. "I'm the *king,* sweetheart. Mattias doesn't tell me what to do."

Felix gave him a disbelieving look.

"Fine." Leo sighed. "Technically I'm in charge, but Mattias has been known to have strong opinions, which he doesn't hesitate to share."

"You said. Your inconvenient voice of reason."

"Yes. That. But as far as *who* I bed is concerned, he doesn't interfere. He understands that there are some things a man should be able to decide for himself. Besides, he'll be so thrilled he doesn't have to come along every time I want to go out riding, he won't care about the other."

Felix gave a shy smile, and his wide brown eyes held a spark of want. "Well, if it's not going to cause an uproar, I'd very much like to do this again."

Leo surged forward at that, rolling them so Felix was under him, and kissed his new bedmate thoroughly in case there was any doubt how thrilled he was with Felix's answer. When Leo pulled back he moved to one side, propping himself on his elbow so he could properly take in the sight of Felix. His hair was a riotous mess, his lips were kiss-plumped, and the smile he wore was wide and genuine. He looked just how Leo liked his bed partners to look—sweaty, satisfied, and smiling—and Leo could have stared at him all day.

However, the last of Felix's seed was drying on the skin of his thighs, itchy and unpleasant, and he didn't imagine it was any better for Felix, who was far messier than he was. He sat up with reluctance and swung his legs over the side of the bed, then walked to the washbasin in the corner of the room to fetch a cloth to clean them up.

When he turned around, Felix was propped up on his elbows staring at Leo's bare backside. "What's that?"

"I don't know what you're talking about," Leo lied, even though he knew *exactly* what had caught Felix's eye.

Felix patted the bed. "Yes, you do. Come here and lie down so I can have a proper look."

"Bossy," Leo grumbled under his breath, but he lay

down on his stomach anyway. Felix ran a hand over the dip of his lower back and down his left arse cheek, coming to rest just above the crease of his thigh and smoothing his thumb over the spot that held his interest. "It's the royal birthmark," Leo said before Felix could ask. "All my family have it."

Felix leaned in closer. "It looks like...a pair of lips."

He pressed a soft kiss of his own to the spot, and Leo shivered. "I've heard that birthmarks are the mark of an angel's kiss."

Felix barked out a laugh at that. "Of *course* you'd think the angels kiss your arse."

"Hush, you. It's deeply significant and proof of my royal lineage. And technically, it's on my upper thigh."

"If you say so," Felix said, "but it looks like your arse to me."

Leo didn't bother to reply, instead rolling over and manoeuvring Felix onto his back, pressing his knees open so he was splayed wide, and running the damp cloth over his skin. Felix let out a soft gasp at the chill of the water, but other than that he didn't protest as Leo cleaned him up. Leo made quick work of it and wiped himself down as well before dropping the cloth to the floor.

Felix yawned and blinked, sleepy-slow, and he looked so tempting that Leo wasted no time in arranging them so that he was curled along the length of Felix's spine. He wrapped an arm around his waist, keeping him close, and whispered, "I think we both need a nap to recover from that, don't you?"

Felix tensed when his probably still-tender arse made contact with Leo's front, but it was a momentary thing before he relaxed in Leo's hold and hummed in agreement, pressing back against him. It didn't take long for his breathing to turn deep and even, and with his body a solid wall of warmth and comfort, Leo was quick to follow him down into sleep.

When he woke it took Leo a moment to become aware of the presence of another body in his bed, but once he remembered, he couldn't help but smile to himself. His delightful groom had agreed to be his bedmate. He took a moment to appreciate the elegant curve of Felix's neck and placed a barely there kiss on the nape. He was just contemplating whether Felix might enjoy getting sucked off in his sleep when there was a tap on the door, followed by another two rapid-fire, and a familiar voice called, "Are you decent, or am I leaving the trays?"

Leo sighed and sat up, running his fingertips down the nape of Felix's neck to rouse him. Felix rolled over and squinted up at him, one eye open. "Whu?"

"Mattias is here with our supper, sweetheart."

Felix sat bolt upright. *"Mattias?"*

"Well, who else was going to bring our trays?" He called out, "We're decent."

Felix went wide-eyed and looked around as if seeking somewhere to hide, so Leo pulled him close and kissed him to distract him from his panic. It seemed to work, but what was shaping up to be a very pleasant kiss was interrupted by Mattias calling out again. "The door's locked."

Leo rolled his eyes. "I *know* it's locked," he called back as he rolled out of bed and pulled his shirt over his head and stepped into his trousers, barely lacing them before opening the door. "You *told* me to keep it locked after that time with the—"

"Don't remind me," Mattias said, walking in with a large tray. He stopped short when he saw who was in the bed. *"Felix?"*

Felix, who had pulled the quilt up to his chin, gave a tiny, embarrassed shrug. "So, um, you don't have to schedule that meeting with the king?"

Mattias looked from one to the other, then back at Leo, who gave a shrug of his own. "I asked, and he agreed."

Mattias set the tray down on the table and sent Felix a look that held a wordless query, and Felix nodded from his nest in the quilts. Mattias folded his arms over his chest, turning a sharp gaze on Leo. "I'm curious as to how, despite assuring me you were staying in your office and dealing with your correspondence this afternoon, you somehow managed to find time to seduce your new groom?"

"Ah. Yes, that. Um, he started it?"

"He…started it,*"* Mattias repeated slowly.

Felix blushed, but then, in a show of courage that only increased Leo's admiration for him, straightened his spine, looked Mattias in the eye, and said, "Actually, I did. And, um"—he took a deep breath—"I—*we'd*—like to do it again?"

"Oh?"

"If…Leo says you don't interfere with his, um, private affairs, but is it really all right? If this is a regular thing?" Felix ducked his head, all his courage apparently departing, and swallowed loudly.

Mattias shook his head in what Leo recognised as fond

resignation. "Of course it's fine. All I ask is that you be discreet and try not to neglect your normal duties in the pursuit of, well, this." He pointed between the two of them, and suddenly Leo was a teen all over again and being led out of the forest while listening to Mattias grumble about his impulsive behavior.

Mattias tended to have that effect when he was serious about something—and it obviously wasn't confined to just Leo. Felix nodded, gripping the edges of the quilt so tightly that his fingertips were white. "I won't, I swear."

Mattias raised an eyebrow. "Actually, I wasn't talking to you, Flick. I know *you* won't duck your responsibilities."

Leo gasped. "Mattias! Are you implying I'm irresponsible?"

Mattias arched one eyebrow at him in reply, and while Leo wasn't completely certain it was an insult, it probably was. He decided to make Mattias squirm a little in retaliation. "I thought you'd be pleased to know that Felix is available whenever I want to ride."

"Oh my gods," Felix muttered and covered his face with one hand, the tips of his ears now scarlet.

"He'll act as my personal guard when I take Blackbird out," Leo continued, pretending he didn't know exactly how that had sounded.

Mattias let out a long, slow breath. "You're talking about appointing him your personal guard?"

Leo gave a bright smile. "Of course. What did you think I meant? His father trained him in weapons and hand to hand, so he's able to protect me. He can accompany me when I go riding instead of half the guard tagging along."

Mattias tilted his head to the side. "That," he said slowly, "actually makes good sense."

"Thank you," Leo said tartly. "Nice to know that as your *ruler*, I'm capable of making the odd good decision. Now if you'll excuse us." He gestured toward the door, eager to have Felix to himself again.

Mattias let out a low chuckle. "I'll leave you to your supper. Goodnight, Leo. Goodnight, Felix."

Once he was gone, Leo fetched the tray and carried it over to the bed, where Felix had let the quilt pool around his waist. He looked considerably more relaxed now that Mattias was gone. "That went better than I thought it would," he admitted, fidgeting with an oat cake.

"I told you there was nothing to worry about. Mattias would never interfere unless you were a spy or an assassin. *Are* you a spy or an assassin?"

Felix shook his head, smiling now.

"Then there's no problem. Now eat something," Leo said encouragingly. "You need to keep your strength up."

"Oh, I do, do I?" Felix asked, his smile widening, making Leo want to kiss him—and do all sorts of other things as well.

"Oh, absolutely," he purred as he pressed a cube of cheese to Felix's lips. "After all, I have you to myself for the rest of the night, and I plan to make the most of it."

## Chapter Seven

When Felix blinked awake, Leo was spooned up behind him, warm and solid, with a hand curled around his hip, and he was nestled in the most comfortable bed he'd ever had the pleasure of sleeping on. He pulled the quilt up around his chin and let himself enjoy it.

It wasn't surprising that Leo was still asleep, since he'd made good on his promise to make the most of their night together. They hadn't fucked in the end, but that was more due to lack of preparation than anything else. There had been no oil to be had anywhere in the room, and the prospect of either calling for some or leaving their bed hadn't appealed to either of them. Leo had briefly tried to convince Felix to go and fetch some, but Felix had refused point blank, citing Mattias's appeal that they be discreet. He'd pointed out that wandering around the castle at near to midnight looking for lubrication was the opposite of that, which had earned him a pout, but Felix had been firm. Fucking would have to wait.

It had turned out not to matter. There was plenty of fun to be had in other ways.

They'd spent time exploring each other's bodies, teasing and touching, sharing gentle kisses and playful nips and more than one orgasm—the king had been able to make Felix come just from teasing at his nipples while Felix rutted against his leg—and afterwards, when they were both at a point where they were too tired for more, they'd curled up together and talked until the wee small hours. Felix had found that Leo was surprisingly down to earth. He'd always assumed that his public persona of a man of the people was a front, but he discovered that Leo genuinely did care about the citizens of Lilleforth.

It reassured him somewhat about his heat-of-the-moment acceptance of Leo's proposition. In truth he hadn't been sure at first if it was a wise move, because he was, first and foremost, in the employ of the castle, and he'd worried that if it all went to hell, it would affect his job. But Leo had looked so hopeful when he'd asked, and Felix had felt like something of a tit for having accused Leo of only wanting him for a bed warmer. Saying no after finding out that he had been wrong felt a little too much like slapping Leo in the face because of his own misconceptions, when really, Leo hadn't set a foot out of line.

And apart from all that? Leo was a clever, witty, interesting man, and there was something about him, a spark of life and an irresistible charm, that drew Felix in and made him eager to spend more time with him, both in and out of bed.

But more time was a luxury he couldn't afford, not right now. He needed to be gone by morning before the maids came to make up the fire and the valet came to tend to the king. He tried to extract himself from Leo's grip without waking him, but the hand on his hip tightened.

Leo's voice was sleep-rough. "Where are you going?"

"I have to get back," Felix said softly. "Discretion means not being here in the morning."

"I don't like discretion if it means you leaving," Leo mumbled, petulant.

"Maybe not, but apart from anything else I have a job to do, and if I'm to do it properly, I need at least a few hours of undisturbed sleep."

Leo kissed the spot at the top of Felix's spine that he'd discovered last night, the one that made Felix shiver. "You make far too much sense for this early in the morning," he grumbled, but he loosened his grip and allowed him to escape. Felix dressed by the dim glow of the last remaining coals, and he was halfway to the door when Leo spoke. "When will I see you again?"

"Whenever you'd like, as long as it doesn't interfere with my work," Felix said, his insides warming at the knowledge that Leo *did* want to see him again.

"Or mine. Despite what Mattias likes to imply, I *do* take my duties as king seriously."

"You know, I believe it. My father wouldn't be as loyal to you otherwise. You just like to *pretend* you're some kind of rebel." On impulse, Felix darted back over to the bed, leaned in, and stole a quick kiss.

"Are you sure you can't stay?" Leo cupped his jaw, and Felix tried not to be distracted by how adorable a sleep-rumpled Leo was.

"I really do have to go. But you know where to find

me." With that, he slipped out the door and down the passageway, following his instincts until he found a corridor he recognised that led him back to the kitchens. It was early enough that it was empty, the work surfaces scrubbed clean, the next day's bread dough proving in a warm spot, and the fires banked for the night. He headed out the door and across the courtyard, past the stables, and up the laneway that led to his own small cottage.

Once there, he changed into his nightclothes and settled into his bed, hoping to get some more sleep in the few hours that remained before dawn. The squeak of the bed frame as he rolled over was somehow comforting, and before long he found himself drifting off. His last thought before he fell asleep was to wonder if Leo would ever come and stay the night here, and if the squeaky frame would keep him awake, but he dismissed it. That wasn't ever going to happen.

He was at the king's beck and call, not the other way around.

∾

Felix was dragged awake by the sound of a rooster crowing and despite his broken sleep, he was refreshed in a way that told him he'd slept the sleep of the well-fucked. Or, in this case, not-quite-fucked. Still, the principle was the same. He'd come more often last night than he could remember doing since he was a youth who had first discovered what his cock was capable of with a little encouragement from his right hand.

And he'd come in the *king's* bed. By the *king's* hand. Because he was the king's lover now.

He let that sink in for a minute.

Thanks to a case of mistaken identity and some shameless flirting, Leopold, ruler of Lilleforth, had chosen him as a bed partner. Felix waited for panic at that revelation to set in, but it was absent. Maybe it was because he had both Leopold's and Mattias's assurances that it was fine for him to consort with the king, or perhaps, on a more practical level, it was simply that Leo was enticing enough that Felix was prepared to take his chances.

Whatever the reason, Felix had no regrets about last night—other than that they hadn't been able to procure a flask of oil.

The cock crowed again with its usual relentless persistence, and Felix shoved back the blankets. He dressed, took a piss, and washed, the cool cloth bringing back memories of last night. He pressed a hand to his arse cheek and yes, there was still the trace of a pleasant ache there. He prodded again, grinning at the memory of it. Perhaps he'd leave today's ride for later, when he was less tender. Leo was obviously a practiced hand, and Felix could appreciate the skill it took to make a spanking sting in just the right way.

He couldn't wait to do it again.

After breakfast, Felix pulled on his boots and made his way to the main stables. He was pleased to see that the floors had been swept, the horses were all groomed, and the tack hanging against the wall gleamed from a thorough cleaning. Obviously, Mother had made Davin earn his keep after all. He moved on to the separate stables that housed

Blackbird and Shadow, approaching Blackbird's stall with an apple extended on his flat palm. She wasted no time stealing the snack.

He laid a hand on her cheek and she leaned into the touch, and Felix spent a few minutes petting her before entering her stall and filling her feed trough. Next he fed Shadow, stroking the horse's thick neck muscles as he murmured, "Did you know Leo's letting me have you as my mount? Isn't that good news?" Shadow nuzzled and huffed out his apparent agreement.

When she'd eaten, Blackbird tossed her head and danced lightly in her stall. Felix gave a soft laugh. "Impatient, girl?"

She tossed her head again in reply and butted against his shoulder, and Felix took the hint. Slipping a halter on her and attaching a lead rope, he guided her out of the stall and let her loose in the adjoining meadow where she trotted off, found a stretch of dirt, and rolled around in it for a few minutes before standing and ambling over to graze in a lush patch of grass.

When he released Shadow into the meadow, the horse quickly found some dirt to roll in as well. If Felix didn't know better, he might have thought they were expressing their displeasure at him abandoning them yesterday afternoon, but no, horses were just like that.

It was fine. He was planning to groom them properly later anyway. For now, he'd leave them to their fun.

He was midway through mucking out Blackbird's stall when there was the rap of knuckles against the door of the stables, and he looked up to find his father leaning there watching him. He paused in his efforts and, wiping a forearm over his brow, walked over to the door, blinking in the bright light. Judging by the way the sun had climbed higher in the sky, more time must have passed while he was working than he'd thought. His father pulled a cloth-wrapped parcel from the depths of his coat and opened it, revealing a roast beef sandwich. Felix took it with a grateful nod.

He was two bites in when his father said, "I thought you might need to keep your strength up, seeing as I heard that you'd spent the night cavorting with the king."

Felix didn't choke on his mouthful but it was a near-run thing, and his cheeks burned. "Nobody was meant to know!"

He'd promised to keep his activities quiet, yet his father had heard about his exploits before midday. Did the whole castle know?

His distress must have been obvious because his father was quick to reassure him. "Relax, son. Mattias felt I should be made aware that there might be some...late night meetings. That's all."

"Oh." That made sense, Felix supposed. Still, it didn't make this any less embarrassing. "Are you here to tell me I shouldn't be doing this?"

His father fixed his gaze on his boots. "Actually, I'm here to make sure you haven't been talked into anything you don't want to do. Just because Leopold is the king, it doesn't mean he gets to command you into his bed."

A warm feeling spread in Felix's chest. The last thing he wanted to talk about was who he was bedding, and the feeling obviously went both ways, but here his father was anyway, pushing his own discomfort aside to make sure Felix wasn't being coerced. His concern was touching, if awkward.

It was Felix's turn to examine his boots. "I, um. I propositioned him, actually."

His father's head snapped up. *"You propositioned the king?"*

"Well, in my defence, I didn't *know* he was the king at the time."

His father gave an exasperated sigh. "Only you could accidentally charm the king into bed, Flick."

"The charming was mutual, I promise."

His father shook his head. "If you tell me you're both in agreement, that's good enough for me. I don't want any details."

"And I will never, ever offer any. Except—" Felix pushed through his own awkwardness, jutting his chin out. "It was meant to be a one-time thing, but, um. Now it isn't."

"I guessed as much." His father's expression did something complicated like it always did when he was deciding whether to say something, and he drew a deep breath. "Flick," he said quietly, "you know this can never be anything more than a tumble in the sheets, don't you? Leopold will have to marry one of his princesses eventually."

"I know that, Dad."

And Felix *did* know. He had no expectation of anything more than a passing dalliance. He and Leo would have a good time, and when Leo tired of him in a week or a month or a year, the invitations to his bedchamber would dwindle away to nothing, and then they'd both pretend there had never been anything between them at all.

That was how these things worked.

His father gave an uncertain smile.

"It's fine," Felix assured him. "He's the king, I'm the hired help, and this is fun, but it's just a fling." He bit into his sandwich in a desperate effort to stop talking about his sex life with his father.

Obviously, Felix wasn't the only one keen to change the subject. "Mattias also said something about you being the king's personal guard?"

Felix swallowed his mouthful of sandwich. "Oh! I'm going to be the king's guard when he goes riding. Since you trained me yourself, he's confident I'm up for the job."

His father raised an eyebrow. "It's a good idea, and I'll take it as a compliment. And *you'll* come down to the training yards at least three times a week to keep you sharp."

Felix grinned. He might not have wanted to be in the Royal Guard per se, but he did enjoy sparring. "I'll find the time."

"Make sure you do." Felix made to step away, but his father held up a hand. "Wait. One more thing." He unbuckled the fastenings of his weapons belt and held it out, complete with a still-sheathed short sword. "Here. If you're the king's personal guard, you'll need a weapon."

Felix took it and fastened it around his waist, the weight reassuring against his hip. He patted the sheath, nodding his thanks.

His father put a hand on Felix's shoulder, an affectionate gesture. "Your mother says come for dinner tomorrow. She thinks it's not fair that I get to see you more than she does."

"I will."

They shared a brief one-armed embrace before Janus took his leave and strode with confidence across the cobblestones, doubtless on his way to knock the latest batch of recruits into shape.

～

Felix took himself up to the kitchens for lunch and when nobody gave him so much as a glance, he concluded that his father was right and his liaison with the king was still a secret. He shifted in his seat and smiled to himself at the lingering ache that reminded him of the night before. He wondered idly if the king was a fan of riding crops.

Once he'd eaten, he made his way back to the stables and leaned on the railings around the yard, enjoying the warmth of the sun on his skin as he watched Blackbird and Shadow meandering across the meadow. The day was bright and cloudless, and the blue of the sky reminded him of Leo and his laughing eyes, which led to him thinking about what his father had said. Given the king's good looks, his sharp wit, and most importantly, the kingdom's port access, Felix didn't doubt that some princess or other would wrangle Leo into a political marriage eventually, though he appeared to be doing a good job of avoiding it so far.

And although Felix knew the king's marriage was inevitable, he couldn't help but hope it didn't happen *too* soon.

Not when they'd just started having fun.

He sighed and stood up straight. Now wasn't the time for daydreaming. He had horses to look after. He clicked his tongue, extending his palms with two halves of a carrot as enticement. Upon hearing him and seeing what he held, Blackbird ambled over for her treat, Shadow following in an imitation of his namesake, and Felix led them back into their stalls.

He started with Blackbird, checking her hooves and running his hands over every inch of her before he set about grooming her properly. It was something both he and the horse enjoyed, and he liked to think it strengthened their bond. He loved the solidity and strength of her, and he soon lost himself in the circular motion of the currycomb against her coat, taking his time to work any dirt loose before brushing her clean and rubbing her down until her coat gleamed.

He brushed out her mane and tail and fed her an apple, and when he was done, he turned his attention to Shadow. The horse was steady, mild-mannered, and a dream to ride, which was why Felix liked him. He repeated the grooming process, then stored the brushes and made sure both horses were settled in their stalls.

He placed his hands on his hips and was just arching his spine to get the knots out of it when out of the corner of his eye he caught movement. A figure was walking toward him and as they got closer, he saw that it was none other than Leopold.

He was dressed in his own clothes today, and Felix took a moment to appreciate the excellent fit of his riding trousers. As Leo approached, his face split in a smile. "Is Blackbird ready to ride? I thought I'd take her out if you're free to accompany me?"

Felix grinned. "I'm always available for you."

Leo's smile widened. "I'm glad to hear it."

There was a small delay in saddling the horses while Leo backed Felix against the wall and kissed him thoroughly. Felix couldn't say he minded, not when he got to run his hands along Leo's muscled back and down over the curve of his arse in return. And once they'd gotten that out of their system, it didn't take them long to get saddled up.

They mounted their horses and Felix closed his eyes for a second and took a deep breath, the scents of straw and sweat and horse filling his lungs, before he gave a light flick of the reins and Shadow moved forward, obedient as always. Leo and Blackbird fell into step beside him, the horses' hooves clattering on the cobbles when they crossed the yard. "Did you have anywhere you wanted to go in particular?" Felix asked.

"I know a quiet spot. Mattias gave me disappointed looks all morning until I dealt with my correspondence, and now I need to clear my head." Leo twitched his reins and picked up his pace to a trot, heading out across the expanse of the meadow towards the distant edge of the woods, and Felix followed suit.

Leo was an excellent rider, confident in his movements and in complete control. Blackbird obeyed his slightest signal, and Leo showed no hesitation in pressing her into a gallop until her hooves went flying over the grass, faster than Felix had ever seen her run, and they raced ahead. Felix spurred Shadow on as well and it didn't take long before he was pulling alongside them—and what he saw took his breath away, because Leo on horseback was a thing of beauty.

His hair was windblown, his shirttails askew, and he looked nothing like royalty at all. He was grinning like a madman, his cheeks rosy from the wind and his face a picture of absolute joy as he leaned forward in the saddle urging Blackbird on. His eyes were alight with exhilaration, and he showed no signs of slowing down anytime soon.

Felix settled in next to him and let Shadow have his head, and together they surged forward, the horses' hooves thundering against the hard-packed soil of the dirt track that led to the woods, the stables becoming an ever-decreasing speck in the distance. Felix's heart thundered in his chest with the sheer thrill of it as they rode and rode and rode.

It was almost a disappointment when Leo straightened in the saddle, causing Blackbird to slow to a trot and then a walk, but Felix knew it was the right move. Shadow's sides heaved with exertion beneath him, and he couldn't imagine Blackbird was any different. He leaned forward and patted the side of his neck. "Shhh, good lad," he said quietly. "We'll let you have a rest, shall we?" Shadow tossed his head and snorted in reply as if to say that yes, a rest would be appreciated.

When Felix glanced over, he saw that Leo had slid from his saddle and was leading Blackbird towards a small grove of trees, petting her nose as he did so and crooning at her.

Felix dismounted and followed, and when he rounded the curve of the path, he was delighted to find that there was a small brook with clear water splashing over rocks and a pleasant clearing with soft-looking grass that was strangely flat in a couple of spots. "Oh, this is nice! I didn't know this was here."

Leo beamed at him, obviously pleased with himself. "I thought you'd like it. It's where I come when I need a quiet place to think, and I mostly have it to myself."

"Mostly?"

Leo indicated the flattened grass. "There's been a time or two when it's been occupied by young lovers seeking their own quiet space, in which case I ride on by and pretend I haven't seen anything." He led Blackbird over the brook and let her drink before he looped her reins over a tree branch and lowered himself onto a patch of greenery. He settled back on his elbows with his legs extended and his ankles crossed and patted the ground next to him in wordless invitation. Felix didn't need to be asked twice.

He let Shadow drink and tethered him, then stretched out beside Leo. It wasn't really any surprise when Leo pressed him flat against the grass before propping himself over Felix and kissing him. Leo was surprising in his tenderness, and they passed the time like that for a little while, trading lazy kisses and letting their hands roam. Felix had hoped that they might take things further, but Leo pulled back with a sigh when his hand bumped against the sheath of Felix's short sword. "We should stop."

"You started it," Felix pointed out, running the tip of his tongue over his lips where they tingled pleasantly.

"I did," Leo agreed, "but I promised Mattias I wouldn't be too long, and I do want to be allowed to do this on a regular basis."

Felix snorted a laugh. "Are you *sure* you're the king and not Mattias?"

Leo stood, extending a hand down to Felix and helping him up. He hesitated, running his thumb over Felix's bottom lip. "Don't think for a second that I'm not tempted to pin you down and take you apart until you're begging right here and now. But I asked you to ride as my bodyguard, not come and dally as my bedmate. Now is not the time nor the place."

The knowledge that Leo valued his skills as much as he admired his body gave Felix a warm feeling in his chest, which almost made up for the lack of kissing and touching. He resisted the urge to ask Leo if he was *sure* they didn't have time to flatten their own patch of grass and instead loosed Shadow's reins and hefted himself into the saddle.

Leo mounted Blackbird with a grace borne of long practice and they meandered back towards the castle in comfortable silence, not racing this time but setting a more sedate pace. It was as the horses ambled into the stable yard that Leo cleared his throat. "I wonder, did you have plans for this evening?"

Felix pulled Shadow to a halt and slid to the ground. "It depends. What did you have in mind?"

Leo dismounted and stepped up close, eyes dark and voice low. "I've spent the entire ride back watching your arse bounce in that saddle, and it's done nothing to diminish my desire to pin you down and do wicked,

wicked things to you. Will you come to my rooms later tonight?"

"Yes, on one condition."

Leo raised an eyebrow in silent enquiry.

Felix grinned. "Make sure there's oil."

## Chapter Eight

The next morning, Leo woke to the first strains of birdsong and stretched out a hand, seeking the man he'd fallen asleep next to. He immediately regretted it when he touched nothing but cold bed linens and a wet, sticky mess. But despite the unpleasant dampness he couldn't hold back a smile, because it was his and Felix's mess, a tangible reminder of the night they'd spent together.

He rolled onto his back and stared at the canopy of his bed, letting himself remember. Felix had arrived at his room long after most of the castle was asleep and proceeded to slip into Leo's bed and make himself at home between the sheets and between Leo's thighs, getting his mouth on Leo's cock and teasing him until Leo was achingly hard.

Felix had laughed, delighted, when Leo had flipped him onto his belly, and when Leo ran a thumb down the crease of Felix's arse, he'd found him already slicked and open.

"Thought I'd save you the bother," Felix had said, grinning, "so you can go ahead and fuck me. Hard."

And Leo had.

It had been glorious, sinking into that warm, welcoming heat, and Felix had let out the most delectable sounds as Leo had ploughed his arse hard and fast. There were few things Leo enjoyed more than a responsive lover, and Felix writhing and panting beneath him, letting out soft grunts and gasps when Leo drove in deep, had soon had him on the edge of release. With one final thrust, hands locked around Felix's hips, Leo had spilled with a low groan, his cock pulsing and his body shaking with pleasure.

Then Leo had rolled them onto their sides and brought Felix to his own release with a deft hand. Afterwards they'd lain there for a little while, tangled together and panting, before Felix had sighed, his contentment obvious, and said, "We can do that again anytime you'd like."

Anytime had turned out to be several hours later, soft kisses turning into a slow, lazy coupling with both of them barely awake, and it had been different from their earlier frenzied fucking, but no less satisfying.

Now that he was slightly more coherent, Leo had vague memories of Felix shaking him awake sometime in the predawn light, whispering that he had to go before placing a soft kiss on Leo's cheek and slipping out the door.

Leo propped himself up, wiping his sticky hand on the bed linens. He wasn't sure why, but Felix leaving before dawn unsettled him despite the fact that this was the way it was always done. The pretty lads came to his chambers, they shared a bed, and then they left. He'd never had the desire for anyone to stay.

He contemplated rolling over and going back to sleep, but after a few minutes of tossing and turning, he was forced to accept that he was far too awake now for that to happen. He sat up with a sigh. Perhaps he could go to his office and deal with the newest crop of paperwork. Then he'd have time to go riding later, now that he wasn't dependent on Mattias to take him. Hiring Felix as his personal guard had been one of his more brilliant ideas, if he did say so himself.

He dressed and headed to the kitchens. Technically he *could* have called for someone to deliver his breakfast, but this would be quicker—not to mention that the baked goods for the day would be coming out of the oven about now, and the thought of warm bread rolls made his mouth water.

For all that he was the king, Leo did like the simple pleasures in life—like fresh bread warming his belly, or a pretty groom warming his bed.

Upon entering the kitchen Leo found a seat where he'd be out of the way of the servants and nodded at the cook, who greeted him with a cursory bob of her head before fetching him a bowl of porridge with honey and dried apple, and two bread rolls topped with curls of butter. Leo devoured it all with gusto before accepting a mug of strong tea that he carried with him to his office before he was tempted to linger in the kitchen and waste his morning.

Once settled at his desk, he worked his way through the inevitable pile of correspondence. Most of it was for show: signing letters of congratulation to subjects who'd achieved some milestone, accepting or rejecting invitations from nearby kingdoms for public engagements, and the odd letter that Mattias felt required a personal reply, such as the poorly spelled appeal from a young man, written in ragged lettering, begging for a place in the Royal Guard and assuring the king that he was strong as an ox and loyal to the king and wouldn't cause any bother.

When such letters had a note from Mattias attached, the answer was always going to be yes.

Leo penned the invitation to join the guard himself, because a letter written in the king's own hand and stamped with the royal seal meant there could be no doubt to the validity of the offer. He put the envelope to one side and felt a small thrill of triumph when he realised that for the first time in weeks, his desk was clear.

Well, *almost* clear.

There, sitting to one side, was the letter from Evergreen informing him of Princess Sophia's impending visit. He picked it up and read it through again. The visit wasn't for a month, so there was time to prepare, and really, refusing wasn't an option without causing offence. Leo sat back in his chair and rubbed at his temple with one hand. Evergreen was by and large a peaceful nation, given over mainly to agriculture. True to its name, the kingdom was nestled in a broad valley with plentiful waterways, decent rainfall, and rich soil, and the lush farmlands supported livestock and provided an abundance of fresh produce. As such, from a strategic viewpoint, even though Evergreen was small, it was important to foster good relations with them.

Leo just had to work out how to stay on their good side without having to marry someone.

He turned the embossed card over and over in his fingers, contemplating his options. He was confident he could safely host the princess and her entourage without it resulting in matrimony. The trick, he'd learned, was to in *no way* indicate he was aware of the expectations of a proposal. It was a strategy that had worked in the past, and there was no reason to think it wouldn't again.

And if he offered a favourable trade agreement, there would be no need for a wedding.

One thing he was certain of—he had no plans to marry anytime soon. He was aware that one day he'd be obliged to choose a bride and produce the required heir, but in the two years since he'd ascended to the throne, he'd succeeded in delaying the inevitable. It wasn't even that he had anything against the parade of princesses and noblewomen sent his way. When he'd been a youth, he'd graced one young lady's bed several times and found it pleasant enough, but it hadn't been what he'd really wanted, and still wasn't.

And he definitely wasn't ready for marriage.

Not when he'd only just acquired a new companion, one who not only shared his tastes in the bedroom, but could match wits with him and make him laugh, and who didn't kowtow to him just because he was the king. He smiled to himself at the memory of Felix grinning and wiggling his arse in invitation and wondered when he could ask him to come back. Not tonight—Leo wasn't so foolish as to think he could take three nights in a row of barely any sleep—but *soon*.

There was a knock at the door and Mattias entered. He looked at Leo, then at the cleared desk, then at Leo again, and broke into a wide smile. "Perhaps you should take lovers more often if this is the result."

Leo flapped a hand at him. "Rude. You know I always do what's required of me."

"Eventually."

Leo ignored the barb. "Now that you're here, we need to hold a banquet for Princess"—he tapped the card—"Sophia of Evergreen. She and her retinue are passing through in a month's time and have asked to visit."

Mattias hummed. "And I'm assuming you're not going to propose to this one either, which is a shame because Evergreen would make an excellent ally."

Leo rolled his eyes. "Which is why I'll invite them to formalise a trade agreement instead."

Mattias plopped himself in the chair on the other side of the desk, then leaned forward and plucked the card from Leo's hand. "My thoughts exactly. I'll start making arrangements for the visit and sort out the banquet. Then we'll draw up some proposals we can present to distract them from your lack of interest in their princess. A month is plenty of time to prepare."

"Thank you." Leo stood and stretched, the cracking of his spine a reminder that he'd been sitting for longer than he'd thought. The envelope on top of the pile caught his eye. "The boy who wants to join the guard. I assume there's a story?" There normally was, when Mattias intervened.

"He's a decent lad. He'll do well," Mattias said with what could only be deliberate vagueness.

Leo waited.

"Fine. There are six sons and three beds and his father's

about to turn him out," Mattias said. "We have room, and he'll train up well."

It was a source of constant amusement to Leo that despite being a part of the fabric of the monarchy for so many years, Mattias still managed to have an ear to the ground when it came to the poorest areas of the city and the desire to help anyone who wanted to find a way out—perhaps because he'd grown up there himself. He had an uncanny knack for finding a suitable place for anyone who needed it. Possibly half the people working in the castle were there on Mattias's recommendation, but it was an arrangement that seemed to work, so Leo didn't look too closely at it. Part of being a good ruler was leaving well enough alone.

He held out the envelope with the invitation. "Will you deliver it yourself?"

Mattias grinned. "I'll take Janus with me to collect him. Some pomp and ceremony will make the boy's day. He'll be the talk of the street for weeks."

"You know, it wounds me that you're so soft-hearted to everyone in the entire kingdom *except* me," Leo teased.

"Well, not everyone in the kingdom is a pain in my arse like you are," Mattias shot back, standing and taking his leave.

Leo laughed and called to Mattias's retreating back, "Just for that, I'm going riding and leaving you to deal with all the arrangements for this damn visit."

He went back to his rooms and changed into his riding clothes, too impatient to wait on his valet, and hurried to the stables, where he found Mother Jones scolding a lad in his teens who was scowling at the ground.

"Hello, Mother. Is Felix around? I wanted to go for a ride."

The lad's head snapped up, his eyes widened, and his mouth dropped open in an *O* of shock. "Shit, you're Leopold!"

Mother gave the boy a cuff around the ear. "Davin!" He sighed and pinched the bridge of his nose. "Apologise to the king!"

The boy's face went bright red and he gave a wobbly bow and blurted out, "Sorry, Your Majesty. I didn't mean to say shit! It's just, why are you here?"

Mother groaned.

Leo looked the boy up and down. He was still at that age where he seemed to be made of elbows and knees, and young enough that he sported a crop of peach fuzz on his cheeks. "Davin, is it? How long have you worked here?"

"Three weeks, Your Majesty."

"He's *been here* three weeks," Mother said. "He's *worked* for maybe half that and idled away the rest."

Leo found himself more amused than anything, but it wouldn't help Mother keep the boy in line if the king was seen to be indulgent, so Leo suppressed his smile and put on his sternest expression. "If you work in my stables, you *work*, understand me? I'll be checking with Mother."

"Y-yes, sire," Davin whispered, curling in on himself and keeping his head bowed.

Mother gave Leo a grateful look. "You wanted Felix, Your Majesty?"

"If he's around."

Mother poked Davin in the chest. "You. Run up to the cottage and get Felix."

Davin scurried off, casting a last glance back over his shoulder like he still couldn't believe *the king* was standing there. As he disappeared up the path, Leo asked, "One of Matty's?"

Mother nodded. "Nice enough, got a bit of charm when he puts his mind to it, but never met a job he couldn't avoid. I don't know where Mattias found him, but he's not one of his usual waifs and strays. I don't think he's ever had to lift a finger in his life."

"Oh?"

Mother snorted. "When he stood in shit on his first day, he asked who was going to clean his boots. Got a hell of a shock when the answer turned out to be him."

Leo laughed. "Well, if anyone can whip him into shape, you can, Mr. Jones."

"Thank you, sire. The chancellor said the same thing." He gave a crooked smile. "And in the meantime, at least Davin's entertaining."

While he waited for Felix, Leo fed Blackbird a handful of apple halves and ran a hand down her cheek, and she nuzzled him back to show her appreciation. It wasn't long before Felix appeared with creases on his face and his hair sticking out at odd angles in a way that suggested he'd been napping. He stopped a very proper three feet away and inclined his head in a respectful bow. "You sent for me, Your Majesty?"

"I'm taking Blackbird out. You'll join me on Shadow."

Felix beamed. "Of course, sire."

Even though Felix was using his title in its proper context, it still sent a shiver up Leo's spine, making him think all sorts of indecent thoughts. He pushed them aside. For now, he had a horse to mount.

The groom could come later.

~

They spent a pleasant afternoon riding. There was no urgency to get back, so they travelled farther than the day before, not stopping except to let the horses rest. Felix was good company, irreverent and entertaining, and it was a long time since Leo had laughed so hard or been so relaxed. Eventually, though, the sun started to dip lower in the sky, and Leo turned Blackbird towards home.

When they got back to the stables, the rest of the horses were grazing in the meadow and there was nobody around, which meant Leo could indulge himself and crowd Felix into a stall and press against him, running his hands down his back and imagining bare skin. "Come and see me tonight?" he said, forgetting for a moment that he wasn't going to ask.

Felix shook his head. "I wish I could, but I've barely slept in two nights. I'm buggered."

"I know. I was there."

Felix snorted. "I'm serious. I have a job to do, and so do you." There was no sting to his words, though. "Tomorrow?"

Tomorrow sounded forever away to Leo, but he gave a reluctant nod. "Fine."

Felix rewarded him with a quick kiss, then reached behind himself and grabbed something and pressed it into

Leo's palms, whispering, "If you're very lucky, I'll be terribly disrespectful, and you'll have to show me my place."

Leo blinked down at the riding crop. He imagined the lovely marks it would leave, stark red against Felix's pale arse, and his cock throbbed in anticipation. He tucked the crop into the side of his riding boot. "Until tomorrow, then."

Felix grinned and shoved him lightly backward. "Tomorrow. Now go and do some work and let me do mine."

Leo left, a spring in his step and a crop tucked in his boot.

∼

It was just before midnight when Felix slipped into Leo's rooms. Leo was already naked and erect, having spent the last hour teasing himself in anticipation. He wasted no time peeling Felix out of his clothing, pausing only to place a series of kisses down the side of Felix's elegant throat before pulling his shirt over his head and running his palms down his torso, following the curve of his muscles. He slid his hands around Felix's back and cupped his arse, giving it a light squeeze. Felix had such pretty, soft skin.

Leo couldn't wait to mark it.

Felix let out a breathy sigh and Leo echoed it before kissing Felix properly, the heat of Felix's soft, welcoming mouth stoking Leo's desire to new heights until he was achingly hard. He backed Felix against the wall and slipped a hand between them to stroke Felix's cock, relishing the way it hardened further against his palm. Felix gave a shaky moan and Leo's own cock throbbed at the sound, slapping against his belly. He stepped back and removed his hand lest he give in to the temptation to stroke them both off then and there.

"You're a damned tease," Felix complained, but it was half-hearted at best.

"Is that any way to speak to your king?"

Felix grinned, his expression pure, delicious insolence. "It is if he's a tease. What are you planning to do about it?" Felix cocked an eyebrow and ran the tip of his tongue over his bottom lip, making it shine in the dim light. He looked delectable, and Leo didn't want to—*couldn't*—wait any longer.

He reached up and gripped Felix lightly around the back of the neck, steering him over to the end of the bed, bending him at the waist, and pressing him into the bedding. "Hands beside your head. Don't move," he growled.

Felix placed his hands where instructed and breathed out, "Yes, sire."

He made such a pretty picture, laid out with his legs spread wide to accommodate his height. Leo took a moment to appreciate the sight before running his hands over the globes of Felix's backside, kneading and working the flesh to warm it up for what was to come.

Felix jerked at the first crack of Leo's hand against his arse, and Leo relished the pink that bloomed across his skin. He rubbed his palm over the spot and Felix moaned softly, arching back into the touch. Leo grinned to himself and followed the first slap with a series of swats that increased in intensity, his blood heating at the way Felix whined and squirmed under his hand.

When the skin of Felix's arse was a delicious, rich red, Leo leaned in and whispered, "Are you ready for the crop, sweetheart?"

Felix tipped his head back, breathing heavily. "Please, sire." He shuffled back slightly and spread his legs farther as if to brace himself.

Heat raced through Leo's veins at the sight in front of him, and he wrapped a hand around his cock and stroked himself in a slow tease, only stopping when the touch threatened to become too much. Leo pressed a soft kiss to the small of Felix's back and picked up the riding crop, then ran the tip lightly up and down Felix's spine, making him shiver.

Next Leo dragged the wide leather tip back and forth lazily across Felix's arse a few times, drawing patterns and letting the anticipation build, and it was only when Felix's breath hitched that he flicked his wrist. The tip connected with Felix's arse, the soft *thwack* a glorious counterpoint to the sound of Felix drawing in a sharp breath. Leo adjusted his grip and let fly again, harder this time, and Felix let out a satisfying squeal, muscles going taut before relaxing again. Leo laid a palm in the centre of his back. "Yes?"

"Gods, yes." Felix moaned. "Make me feel it."

It was all the permission Leo needed.

He delivered a series of quick hits, his heart racing with excitement as the tip of the crop snapped again and again, leaving fresh welts against Felix's already reddened backside. Felix squirmed and arched and whimpered most delightfully and Leo's blood heated, his arousal heightening and his cock leaking more with every slap of leather on skin.

Leo dragged the length of the crop across the crease where Felix's arse met his thigh in a gentle back-and-forth motion, a threat and a promise. Then, unable to contain himself, he gave one firm whack with the shaft, right across the meatiest part of Felix's arse cheeks.

Felix howled, a single red stripe blooming on his skin, but he didn't ask Leo to stop, and it was so satisfying that Leo didn't hesitate to do it again. At the second blow, Felix threw his head back and gave a choked cry. His spine arched and his hips stuttered forward as he tensed, gasping as he came, before slumping against the bedding, his breathing heavy and his body lax.

The sight of him lying there with his arse spanked red, sprawled out across Leo's bed, made a surge of possessiveness rise up in Leo's chest, a desire to claim the boy as his. His cock throbbed like a heartbeat at the thought, threatening to spill without a touch. He cast the crop aside and stepped into the space between Felix's spread thighs, desperate to reach his release.

It didn't take much—a fist around his aching cock, a few urgent strokes, and he was overcome, his balls drawing up tight. Pleasure flooded through him, and he came in long spurts over Felix's bare skin, rosy flesh painted white.

Leo's toes curled against the rug and he shuddered as his orgasm racked him. He slid his softening length up and down the cleft of Felix's arse, groaning at the heat radiating from the spanked flesh, and draped himself along Felix's spine. Felix let out a contented sigh from beneath him.

Once he'd caught his breath, Leo eased a hand under Felix and helped him stand. Felix let his head loll backward against Leo's shoulder, his eyes closed and a satisfied smile on his face.

"Was that what you wanted, my delightful boy?" Leo asked. He was fairly certain of the answer, but he liked to check.

Felix gave a soft laugh. "Oh yes. We're definitely doing that again."

∽

They fell into a pattern.

Every second night, sometimes two nights running if Leo was particularly persuasive, Felix would visit his rooms, and for a few hours they'd indulge themselves. Sometimes it was fast and rough, and other times they curled up close, making love slow and lazy, and fell asleep still tangled together. Sometimes they used the crop.

Leo continued to wonder how he'd gotten so lucky.

Their arrangement remained mostly hidden, Felix's demeanour giving nothing away. His manner was purely professional if there was anyone else around to see him. When they were alone, though? He'd be downright disrespectful, joking and outright *laughing* at Leo's expense, and then he'd arch one eyebrow, give a wicked grin, and say something like, "Oh dear. I do believe I've forgotten my place."

Leo would growl, "Come up to my rooms tonight and I'll remind you." And that night he'd bend Felix over his lap and spank him as he squirmed and begged until his arse was the colour of ripe summer cherries and just as tempting, and Leo would admire the sight while he fucked him.

"Do you think this potential bride likes the slap of leather?" Felix teased him one evening as Leo applied a cool cloth to his heated skin after a particularly vigorous session with the crop.

Hearing Felix talk about him marrying did strange things to Leo's insides, and he didn't think twice before saying, "Oh, I don't intend to propose."

Felix eased himself up on his elbows and looked back over his shoulder. "You say that, but maybe you'll meet your match and she'll manoeuvre you into it."

Leo pinched his arse—partly in reprimand, partly just to hear him yelp. "You have no faith in me. I've had enough practice by now that I'm an expert at seeming to be unaware of any intentions towards me. I shall remain untethered and available to swat your troublesome rump, I assure you."

He laid a light swat on said rump just to make his point.

Felix laughed, but Leo didn't miss the look of relief that flitted over Felix's face, and he took some comfort in that fact that if Leo was enjoying their liaison more than he should, well, at least he wasn't the only one.

There was one memorable night where *Felix* was the one who did the fucking. There were no words for how it felt when Leo straddled Felix and eased down onto his length. Felix's cock filled him perfectly as Leo rode him until his breath was ragged and his thighs shook. They both agreed it was an experience worth repeating, and though his arse ached all the next day, Leo considered it worth it.

Felix always left while it was dark, and Leo never asked him to stay...no matter how tempting it was.

And while Mattias might have joked about it, taking a lover—*this* lover—was doing wonders for Leo's day-to-day schedule. Leo couldn't ride if he had work to do, and no riding meant no Felix, so he made it his business to be free most afternoons. He'd go to the stables and Felix would be leaning against Blackbird's stall with Blackbird and Shadow saddled and ready to go. They'd spend a couple of hours riding, sometimes stopping in the grove and flattening the grass as they rolled around together kissing and touching, and Leo wasn't sure if it was the riding or the sex or both, but he couldn't remember being happier.

Except for *this* week.

This week, he'd barely seen Felix. With preparations in full swing for the impending visit, the castle was a hive of frantic activity, and Leo hadn't had so much as half an hour to himself, let alone the time or energy to summon Felix to his rooms.

And Leo *knew* it was temporary, and he *knew* it was important to make sure this visit went off without a hitch, and that the trade agreements would benefit the entire kingdom, and that putting his own wants to one side was all part of being the king.

He *knew* that.

He just hadn't expected to miss his pretty groom quite so much.

## Chapter Nine

Felix breathed deeply, enjoying the crisp morning air as Blackbird trotted across the wide expanse of meadow. The days were growing warmer, so he'd decided to ride before the heat of the day. He'd been astride for long enough that there was an ache in his thighs, but he didn't really mind. Blackbird needed her exercise and Felix was happy to take her out, what with Leo being so busy.

Of course, Leo wasn't the only one who was busy. The entire main stables had been in a flurry of activity preparing for the influx of visitors and their horses, and even Davin had managed to put in several days' hard work, though he had complained loudly the entire time. They were as ready as they could be, which meant Felix was free to take Blackbird out.

The gates of the stable yard came into view. As they entered, Blackbird tossed her mane and slowed to a walk, allowing Felix to lead her inside with no fuss. He let her eat and drink before he set about brushing her, and it wasn't long before he was done, running a hand over a freshly groomed flank. He tried not to look at Leo's empty saddle on its stand, a stark reminder of the king's continued absence.

*Eight days.*

It had been eight days since Felix had seen Leo, and he missed the king more than he was willing to admit. Felix wasn't stupid, and he knew that he and Leo couldn't ever be anything more than they were, and that he'd have to give the king up eventually, but that didn't stop the ache in his chest.

The thing was, Felix mused as he cleaned and stored the grooming equipment with a sigh, the more time he spent with Leo, the more he found himself enamoured of him—and not just for his excellent spanking technique and his ability to fuck Felix through the mattress.

Leo listened to him like he *mattered*, and at least half their time in bed was spent talking and laughing, which wasn't something Felix had ever encountered with his previous lovers. He'd come to the realisation over the last week that, as inconvenient as it was, he might possibly be fonder of his idiot monarch than he'd first thought.

*Stupid*, he chided himself.

It didn't matter what Felix thought and felt. It didn't matter that despite his father's warning, he was pining like a fool.

Leo was the *king*, and as such, duty would always come first.

Felix just had to remember that, enjoy what they had while he could, and put aside the ridiculous fantasies that had started to creep into his dreams—the ones where Leo and he just...kept being lovers, and nobody needed an heir, and there wasn't a princess in sight.

Blackbird flicked her tail and stamped impatiently, dragging him out of his thoughts. Felix led her outside and released her, and she trotted over to where Shadow was waiting for her under one of the trees. Tomorrow, he decided, he'd take Ollie with him and let him ride Shadow as reward for the effort the lad had put in during the week. Ollie was only fifteen and a reserved soul, but he had a natural aptitude for horses and was eager to please—and unlike Davin, he didn't slip away to spoon with the kitchen maids when he should have been working.

Felix wished *he* could slip away for some unscheduled spooning, but he didn't hold out much hope of that happening for at least another week, not with the visitors here—and if Leo was coerced into proposing, it probably wouldn't happen at all. He had a feeling that the king's betrothed might take a dim view of sharing her future husband with a mouthy commoner who worked in the stables.

~

The visitors arrived just before noon in a whirlwind of noise and activity with a procession of carriages and carts and staff, and the next few hours were taken up helping Mother, his grooms, and the stable boys feed and house the various mounts and get them settled. Felix was glad of the distraction if he was honest, because at least it stopped the unpleasant squirming in the pit of his stomach when he thought about Leo spending time with the princess.

Gods, Leo would have to be all pomp and ceremony and formal robes for an entire week. It would be torture for him. Felix had no doubt he'd manage it, but he was also certain that Mattias would be forced to listen to Leo's petulant grumbling about the need for footwear and manners. He wondered if Mattias would find it as entertaining as Felix did when Leo pouted. He wished that he could be the one Leo was complaining to, just so he could mock him until Leo put him over his knee.

He shoved the thought aside. His job this week was to take care of the horses, and Leo's job was to take care of the kingdom.

It was just how things were.

He stepped back, surveying the controlled chaos as the last of the horses were fed, watered, and stabled. It had taken a decent chunk of the afternoon, but with everyone pitching in, it was done. He nodded approvingly at Davin, who was currently topping up the feed troughs in the stalls, and, probably swept along in the excitement of the new arrivals, was working harder than Felix had ever seen him. "Well done, Davin."

Davin beamed at him. "Thank you, sir. Did you see the princess? I did. She's got red hair like it's on fire, and she's only a tiny little thing, but she's so—" He made a curving in and out motion with his hands in the air to indicate exactly *what* the princess was. "I'd have her any day of the —ow!" Davin turned and glared at Mother, who'd clipped the back of his head with a broad palm.

Mother glared right back, hands on his hips and chin

jutting out. "She's *royalty*, Davin, not one of your kitchen girls! Have some respect!"

Davin hunched his shoulders up around his ears. "I'm just saying, Leo would have to be mad to let this one go."

Mother rolled his eyes. "*His Majesty King Leopold*, lad. And it's not for us to speculate, is it? It's for us to take care of the horses and keep our mouths shut."

"Sorry," Davin muttered, dropping his gaze to the floor and rubbing the back of his head.

Felix swallowed the sudden lump in his throat, and it became a lead ball lodged in the pit of his stomach. What if Davin was right? What if Leo found Sophia too tempting to pass up?

"You all right, Flick? You've gone all pale." Mother's brow creased in concern.

"Fine," Felix managed to say. "I just need some air." He pushed his way past them and walked outside, resting his elbows on the wooden railing and taking a deep breath as his eyes stung for no reason.

Except that was a lie. He knew why they stung.

He thought back to the night when Leo had said that he had no intention of proposing. He'd assured Felix that he'd turned down enough potential matches by now that he was an expert at it, and it was a comfort that Felix had clung to, because apparently when it came to the king he was a romantic fool.

But the reality of the thing was, Leo *couldn't* keep avoiding marriage. And if Sophia was as beautiful as Davin said, and Evergreen was as important as everyone else said, Leo might not *want* to get out of proposing. He could easily change his mind, and Felix honestly wouldn't blame him. The future of Lilleforth was more important than any casual fling. Felix knew that.

It didn't make it hurt any less.

Felix blinked back the wetness blurring his vision, exhaled noisily, and told himself he was being ridiculous. He was lucky he'd gotten to warm Leo's bed at all, let alone for an entire *month*, and if Leo *did* decide to wed, then mooning over him wouldn't do a lick of good. No, Felix was going to have to be an adult about this and pretend it didn't affect him at all.

He ran a forearm over his eyes to get rid of the dampness there, and when he lowered his hand, he was just in time to see a small figure running towards the stable yard. As they came closer, Felix recognised Pip, one of the kitchen boys, short legs flying like he was being chased. When he saw Felix, the boy waved an arm, lips moving even though he was still out of earshot.

Felix waved back and Pip headed straight for him, coming to a halt. Pip's chest heaved like a bellows as he gasped in air, and Felix waited till he'd caught his breath before asking, "What is it, Pip?"

"Message…from…His Majesty, sir," Pip gasped out.

"What's the message?" Felix asked, his heart beating inexplicably faster.

"He said…said he wants to ride. With the princess. An' he wants you to come with him as his guard. Said be ready in an hour." Pip blew out a long breath, obviously relieved at having delivered his message successfully and unaware of the turmoil now taking up residence in Felix's chest.

Leo wanted to *ride?* With the *princess?*

That didn't seem like the behavior of someone keeping

a prospective spouse at bay. Unless she was terrible around horses, in which case it might be Leo's way of discouraging her affections. Although, having seen the picture Leo presented on horseback, Felix couldn't imagine it doing much to dissuade her.

*Not my concern,* Felix reminded himself, and turned his attention back to Pip. "Tell His Majesty I'll be ready and waiting."

~

Davin hadn't been lying. Princess Sophia was *breathtaking.*

Her hair was a magnificent shade of copper that the afternoon light transformed into a glorious riot of reds and golds, gleaming under the sun's rays. She had delicate features and milky white skin, and she was indeed tiny, but her gaze was sharp and there was nothing weak or milquetoast about her—rather she seemed like the sort of woman who would run a man through with a pike without blinking, if the occasion called for it.

Felix felt he could have liked her under different circumstances.

As it was, though, he couldn't quite shake the seed of jealousy that sprouted in his gut, and it wasn't helped by the fact that Leo had barely acknowledged him. He didn't even look Felix in the eye when he informed him that he and Sophia—because they were already close enough that titles didn't apply, *apparently*—wished to have a private conversation, and he'd appreciate it if Felix and the guardsman appointed to the princess could maintain enough distance to ensure their privacy. Felix, for his part, had bowed his head and said, "As you wish, Your Majesty." He was fairly certain he'd managed to sound sincere.

He wasn't sure if it made things better or worse when the guardsman in question turned out to be his father, but it made sense, he supposed. Who better than the captain of the guard to watch over an honoured guest?

Leo and Sophia rode out ahead, and Felix noted that Sophia gave the appearance of an experienced rider, sitting comfortably in the saddle. More than that, she'd taken the time to whisper soft words to her horse, a pale grey filly, and stroke her nose before mounting, and the affection between them was obvious.

They set a sedate pace, meandering across the lush green fields, and Felix, with his father riding alongside, maintained a suitable distance—far enough back that he couldn't quite make out what they were saying but close enough to act should there be a need. Felix felt the tension in his shoulders ease just from being on horseback and out in the open under the warmth of the afternoon sun. He let out a soft sigh.

At that moment the air was filled with a tinkling laugh, and Felix looked up to see Sophia with her head thrown back. "Leo, you say the *wickedest* things!" She giggled, obviously entertained. Leo, for his part, was wearing a satisfied smile, and Felix kind of wanted to push him off his horse.

"Leo, you're so *funny!*" he mimicked under his breath. He possibly pulled a face.

"All right there, Flick?" his father asked quietly.

"I'm fine," he lied, still scowling.

"Uh-huh." His father gave a gentle tug on his reins and stopped his horse.

"What are you doing? We're meant to be guarding, not dawdling." Felix slowed, Shadow moving restlessly.

"We can guard just fine from another five feet back, but this way Leo and his guest won't see the face on you," his father said under his breath. "Pull yourself together and do your job, son."

Felix slumped in the saddle. His father was right.

He huffed out a breath, did his best to school his features into something pleasantly neutral, and flicked the reins for Shadow to move forward—and just in time, because Leo had also halted and was craning around in his saddle. "Flick?" he called, his brow creased. "Something wrong?"

"No, sire. Just finding my seat," Felix said, giving a nod and ignoring the way his chest squeezed at the use of his nickname.

The princess leaned in close and said something to Leo that had his eyes widening before he nodded and muttered something back that had them both laughing.

*Do your job. Do your job. Do your job.*

Leo had said he had no plans to propose, but if that had changed, well, shouldn't Felix at least be glad that the new queen was beautiful and clever and able to make Leo laugh? Maybe Leo could even be happy.

*Leo's already happy—with you,* a treacherous voice whispered.

Felix ignored it, fixing his eyes on the centre of Leo's back as they rode on and doing his best to ignore the interactions between Leo and the princess. They'd asked for privacy, and he was going to give it to them. He wasn't going to tie himself up in knots just because someone else was making Leo smile.

Mercifully it wasn't long before Leo turned back towards the stables, and Felix whatever the couple—and didn't *that* word make his gut curl?—had wanted to talk about had apparently been resolved to their satisfaction, if the broad smiles they were both wearing was any indication.

It was a relief when Leo and Sophia dismounted and handed over their reins, because it meant Felix didn't have time to think too hard. He busied himself with grooming, feeding, and watering the horses and taking extra care of the princess's filly—partly from professional pride, and partly because she really was a sweet little horse. By the time he was done, the hot flare in his blood, which he was forced to acknowledge as jealousy, had settled into a low simmer. It was probably as good as he could hope for.

His father had stayed, tending his own mount, and before he left, he bumped shoulders with Felix. "I know you don't want to hear it, but she's not the worst match for him."

"You're right," he said. "I don't want to hear it."

His father gave him the look he reserved for idiots. "You need to, though."

Felix leaned against the fencing, arms wide and chin resting against the wooden rail. "I know."

His dad rubbed between his shoulder blades, a comforting gesture Felix remembered from when he was a child. It was soothing in its familiarity, and it helped a little.

"I'll be fine," he mumbled into the railing. "We're just having fun. It's not like I have feelings for him, right?"

His father didn't dignify that with a reply, just patted Felix on the back once more before he walked away.

∼

Felix tossed and turned on his bed, unable to settle. He decided he was blaming the quantity of cheese he'd consumed with his dinner. He huffed and sat up, punching at his pillow like it was somehow responsible before trying once again to get comfortable. He was tired and he needed to sleep because the rest of this week was going to be busy, but his brain insisted on replaying images of Leo and Sophia laughing. and Leo gazing at Sophia with admiration. Felix scowled at the thought of her delicate laugh and exquisite features, features that any man would admire, were he inclined that way.

And Leo *was* inclined that way—or had been, in the past. He'd told Felix about a dalliance with a young noblewoman in his youth. So conceivably, Sophia *could* be an ideal match, which meant that at tomorrow's banquet, Leo would probably propose.

Felix punched his pillow again.

He was staring up into the darkness when there was a soft tap at the door. He tilted his head, unsure if he was hearing things, but there it was again. *Tap-tap-tap-tap.*

He lit the lantern next to the bed and made his way over to the door, opening it the barest crack only to see Leo waiting there. He gave a hesitant smile when he saw Felix, and Felix's heart flip-flopped in his chest. "Can I come in?" Leo whispered.

Felix couldn't hold back a smile at seeing Leo, despite questioning the reason for the late-night visit. He opened the door fully and then Leo was pushing inside, crowding up close and tangling his hands in the front of Felix's nightshirt as he shoved him against the wall and dragged him in for a kiss. Felix responded instinctively, lips parting to allow Leo's tongue entrance as he licked his way inside his mouth in a way that was as familiar as breathing. Leo kissed him thoroughly, and when he pulled back, his eyes were bright. "Hello, sweetheart."

Felix swallowed around the lump in his throat at the pet name. "Not that I'm not happy to see you, but it's late. What are you doing here?"

He waited for Leo to tell him he was getting engaged, that this was one final goodbye, but instead, Leo trailed his fingertips down Felix's cheek. "I *missed* you," he said with a quiet tenderness that had Felix's heart racing. "Obviously. So I waited until dinner was done—gods, it dragged on tonight—and slipped away. Aren't you glad to see me?"

The tightness in Felix's chest eased the tiniest bit. "Always." He couldn't help adding, "But aren't you meant to be charming your future wife right now?"

Leo huffed. "I *told* you, I have no intention of marrying Sophia."

It shouldn't have been as much of a relief as it was. "But you took her riding," Felix said, hating how it sounded like an accusation but unable to help himself. "You don't take anyone riding."

*Except me.*

Leo rolled his eyes. "That was her idea, not mine. She said she had things she wanted to tell me without half the court listening in. And what she *wanted* to tell me was that she has no intention of marrying me, so I shouldn't bother to propose. She's happy to set up a trade treaty, whatever her idiot brother thinks. He's the one who wants her married off." Leo stopped to press a kiss to the hollow of Felix's throat before he murmured, "She also said I should take some time to visit you tonight and fuck the jealous scowl off your face."

Felix drew in a sharp breath. "She *knows?*"

Leo shrugged and slid his hands around Felix's back, hitching up his nightshirt and running his hands over Felix's bare arse. "I told her."

Felix froze. "Really?"

Leo hesitated before amending his statement. "Well, before she told me she wasn't interested in marrying, I was trying to let her down gently. I told her I have someone I care for, and she figured out that it was you. She's very observant."

*Someone I care for.*

On hearing that, warmth spread through Felix's chest and relief flooded his veins. Leo *cared* for him. It was as much as he could hope for, given their respective positions.

He felt the smile spreading across his face and he leaned in and pressed their foreheads together. "I...care for you too."

Leo rewarded him with a soft kiss, the barest brush of lips, before burying his face in the curve of Felix's neck. "I'm glad to hear it," he murmured, his warm breath ghosting against Felix's skin. He pulled back and, with that wicked smile that Felix had come to know so well, said, "So, how about it, sweetheart? Shall we take the princess's advice?"

Leo gave Felix's arse a light squeeze and his breath hitched as arousal ran through him, liquid heat beneath his skin. He'd thought he might not get to have this anymore, but here they were, and it didn't seem like anything had changed after all. He steered Leo backward towards his bed —the one that squeaked, the one that wasn't anywhere *near* fit for a king, except just for tonight, maybe it was— and, in the absence of anything clever to say, settled for a simple, heartfelt, "Please."

## Chapter Ten

Leo lay in Felix's narrow bed sometime in the early hours of the morning with Felix's arm slung over his waist. He was naked, sweaty, and loose-limbed after a spectacular orgasm, and sleep was threatening to drag him under. He knew without a doubt that he had to leave, before he succumbed to the temptation to stay the night and bask in Felix's closeness.

He attempted to move, but Felix let out a sleepy whine and tightened his grip, pulling Leo back into his embrace. "Stay," he mumbled against Leo's hair.

There was nothing Leo would have liked more, but he knew better than to think it was possible. Sneaking out at night and coming back early? That was acceptable—barely. Not being in his bed when his valet came to wake him, though? Tongues would wag, word would spread, and there was every possibility it would be seen as a slight against his supposed intended, and he had no desire to create a diplomatic incident just because he'd fucked his lover so thoroughly that they'd both fallen asleep.

He pulled Felix's arm away and swung his legs over the side of the bed, stretching his arms over his head and resolutely not lying back down, no matter how much he wanted to. "I have to go, darling. Discretion means not being here in the morning."

Felix scrunched up his nose and opened one eye, then propped himself on his elbow. "I suppose it does. But can I—" He leaned across and fumbled with something, and a moment later soft lamplight flooded the cottage. Felix bit his lip. "That's better. I just—I wanted to see you," he said quietly. "To remember how good you look in my bed."

An unexpected wave of affection bubbled up in Leo's chest at that. "I can always come back."

Felix tilted his head to one side and gave an uncertain smile. "You'd come back? I mean, the bed's far too small, and it squeaks."

"Yes, but I don't mind a squeaky bed, not if you're in it." Leo was surprised to find it was the truth. He'd put up with a wobbly frame and thin mattress if he got to spend time with Felix.

Felix's smile blossomed into something more genuine, and he reached out and traced a hand across the small of Leo's back. "Are you sure you can't stay longer?"

Leo stood, dragging on his clothing and his boots. "I wish I could, but you know how this works." He leaned across the bed and cupped Felix's face in one hand, kissing him gently before straightening up. "As it is, I don't know when I can see you again. The next few days are busy. Talks, treaties, entertaining our guests, the banquet..." He sighed.

"You have your job to do, and I have mine," Felix said,

his voice soft. "It's fine, Leo. I am grateful you came to see me tonight, though."

"Pure selfishness on my part, I assure you," Leo said lightly. "I'm far too impatient to wait an entire week to get my hands on that delightful arse."

The corners of Felix's mouth quirked up in a smile. "Of course. You always were entitled."

Leo huffed out a laugh, then kissed Felix once more before walking out the door and into the darkness. Leaving was harder than he'd thought, and he wondered how Felix was able to do it night after night. As he made his way through the shadows back to the castle, he let out a jaw-creaking yawn and was reminded that he was expected to rise early tomorrow for the official welcome breakfast for his guests.

Still, he reflected, at least he'd managed to steal this one night in the middle of the organisational chaos of the visit. He'd *missed* Felix, more than he'd thought he would.

It had almost been a relief when partway into their ride, Sophia had pointed out, eyes bright and knowing, that his groom was jealous. Then she'd suggested Leo should probably do something about that.

He'd been more than happy to take her advice.

By the time he made it back to the castle and up to his rooms, stripped out of his clothes, and rolled into his bed, he could barely keep his eyes open, but there was a well-sated heaviness to his limbs, and the restlessness that had buzzed under his skin over the last few days had all but disappeared. He felt more settled than he had for days, and he didn't think it was just the sex, as good as that had been.

No, it was being with Felix that had unwound all his

tension, the boy seemingly able to smooth out the hitches and wrinkles in his knotted-up nerves as easily as he brushed the tangles from Blackbird's mane.

And maybe he'd feel the lack of sleep later, but he couldn't bring himself to regret staying awake, not with the taste of his boy's spend lingering in his mouth, and not while the memory of Felix laughing as he lavished kisses on Leo's birthmark, teasing him about having an arse blessed by the angels, was still so fresh.

His last waking thought was that his boy was utterly disrespectful—and Leo adored him for it.

~

"Thank the gods this visit is almost over." Leo tugged at the sleeves of the long, fur-trimmed crimson robe that he was wearing. It was heavy and uncomfortable and he couldn't wait to get out of it, and the banquet hadn't even started yet. "I've almost run out of good manners and patience."

Mattias made a noise that might have been sympathetic if it were coming from anyone else. "I know. Politeness is taxing to your contrary nature. But your guests leave in the morning, and you can go back to being your normal, cranky self."

"I'd say you were being rude, but I'm actually too tired to argue with you," Leo said with a sigh. "I'm exhausted from avoiding discussions about when I'm going to propose to Sophia with Prince Stephan. How can Sophia be so clever and her little brother be such a dunce?"

"He's certainly finding it hard to accept that you have

no intention of making a match," Mattias said, "but luckily he doesn't have any sway in the matter."

Prince Stephan, Sophia's younger brother, had spent the week dropping none-too-subtle hints about how a marriage between Leo and Sophia would create one of the most powerful alliances on the entire continent and narrowing his eyes at Leo when he avoided the topic of conversation. Stephan was almost painfully insistent that there be a match between the kingdoms, so much so that in a fit of pique four days into the visit, Leo had grumbled to Mattias that he was going to propose to Stephan instead, just to shut him up.

Mattias had simply raised an eyebrow and said, "And what will you do if he accepts?"

The idea of Leo and Stephan was laughable anyway, because if there was one thing Leo had no patience for, it was idiots—and Prince Stephan truly was an idiot. Although he shared his sister's flaming red hair and well-formed features, he did not share her intelligence. If he had, he would have recognised the trade proposals Mattias and Leo were offering as the boon they were, instead of remaining stuck on the idea that his sister would marry the king.

Still, tomorrow their visitors would leave, and life would go back to normal. Leo couldn't wait. It had been a long week, the days filled with meetings and politics and treaty negotiations, and the evenings taken up with long, pointless dinners where he and Sophia sat together and engaged in polite conversation and Leo watched the bards and troupes of acrobats and jugglers with a fake smile plastered in place.

He might have enjoyed the entertainment more, except he was too busy wishing he was in a certain small cottage with a certain long-limbed groom, engaging in some acrobatics of their own.

He took solace in the knowledge that Sophia wanted to marry him even less than he wanted to marry her. The irony of it was, that as he'd gotten to know Sophia, it had become apparent that she was someone he *could* have settled down with, given her wit and charm—except neither of them were interested in each other that way, which was frankly a relief.

"Leo? Are you wool-gathering again?" Mattias's voice cut in. "I said, make sure you wear this." He held out Leo's hated coronet.

"*Really?*"

Mattias muttered something under his breath about difficult children and shoved the coronet forward at Leo, who knew better than to argue. He ducked his head enough that Mattias was able to settle the coronet in place, brushing his fingers through Leo's curls to make them sit properly before giving a satisfied nod. "There. You look every inch a ruler, sire."

Leo poked his tongue out, but he was secretly pleased that he came up to scratch. It was professional pride, not vanity.

Mattias himself looked particularly well-turned-out in tight black trousers, matching boots that had been polished until they shone, a fitted linen shirt that emphasised his long, lean frame, and a deep blue jacket that made his eyes gleam like sapphires. Leo felt a nostalgic echo of his childhood crush. "You look rather fine yourself, Chancellor," he said with a raised eyebrow. "Maybe you'll finally meet a woman who can tolerate you, dressed like that."

Mattias laughed and poked his own tongue out, but Leo noted his cheeks were tinged with pink, which was unlike him. "Come on. They're waiting for us in the Great Hall," Mattias said and led the way downstairs.

∽

The Great Hall had been decorated for the occasion, which was exactly as lavish as expected. The colourful tapestries that hung from the walls were, for once, free of dust and cobwebs, and the walls gleamed under the illumination of lanterns set into sconces in a way that suggested the stone had been scrubbed within an inch of its life.

The room wasn't the only thing that gleamed. Every noble family from Lilleforth was represented and, like Mattias, the guests had all made an effort to look their best in honour of visiting royalty. Leo took a moment to be glad that Mattias had insisted he wear his coronet and robe.

The evening passed without incident, the wine flowing freely as the guests were plied with course after course of fine food, and Leo spent his time at the king's table greeting anyone who made their way up to him and ensuring he made plenty of flattering comments about his visitors. It was mind-numbing, but he'd done it before, and he caught Mattias giving a tiny approving nod every time Leo went out of his way to assure his guests that it was *such* an honour to host the court of Evergreen.

Once the food had been cleared, the musicians started

to play a jaunty tune, and Prince Stephan was less than subtle when he declared, "And of course you'll dance with my sister, Your Majesty?"

"Of course," Leo said, standing and extending a hand to Sophia. She finished her glass of wine before she gave a small nod of her head and took the proffered hand. Leo led her out to the open space and led her in a simple two-step. Other couples soon joined them, and Leo found that he was enjoying himself more than he'd expected. Sophia was rather fetching in an emerald-green gown and light on her feet as they danced, as was Leo. Her cheeks were rosy, but whether from the dancing or the wine she'd consumed, Leo couldn't say.

When the dance came to an end, Sophia's gaze flicked to the side and Leo followed it, only to find her brother watching them, his brow creased. Sophia gave Leo a bow and he mirrored her action, and she used the resulting closeness of her mouth to Leo's ear to murmur, "I think he's finally realising his hopes of a wedding are in vain."

"I should hope so," Leo whispered back, "since we've been quite clear all along."

The music started up again and they resumed dancing. "My brother has always been oblivious to that which he didn't want to see," Sophia said with a sigh, "but we just have to get through tonight without being manoeuvred into an arrangement." Her mouth quirked up. "I'm sure your groom would have something to say about you getting betrothed. Besides," she confided, her face flushing darker and her voice low, "I find my eye drawn to another."

"You mean there's a better royal match than me? Impossible!" Leo teased.

"He's not even royalty. He's a mere knight, although an uncommonly handsome one," she said with another sigh. "And my brother will disapprove, I have no doubt. But I know who I want, and I mean to have him—that is, if he'll have *me*."

"Anyone who doesn't jump at the chance to wed you is an idiot," Leo said.

Sophia gave a sharp smile. "So, what does that make you then, Your Majesty?"

Leo laughed. "Someone who's not nearly clever enough to keep up with you. I hope your knight is quick-witted as well as handsome."

"Oh, he is," Sophia said, her smile widening as the music slowed and the dancing stopped. "And now we should find other partners, lest my brother gets his hopes up again."

"Good idea," Leo said, bowing once more. He looked about and spotted Mattias standing under a lantern, clutching his goblet tightly and watching them. He waved him over and Mattias was at his side in an instant. "You needed me, sire?"

"Yes, Chancellor. Princess Sophia requires a dance partner."

Mattias's eyes widened just a fraction before he turned his attention to the princess. He gave her a dazzling smile, and she returned it. "Would you care to dance, Your Highness?" Mattias asked, bowing low.

"That would be lovely," Sophia said, a soft note to her voice. Mattias positioned his hands at her waist in a manner that wouldn't raise any eyebrows, the music picked up again, and they were off.

Leo stepped out from among the dancers and made his way to the side of the room, only to find Stephan approaching. He gave a small nod as the man came to a halt in front of him. "Stephan."

"Your Majesty." Stephan's eyes flicked to the dance floor and back to Leopold. "Do you tire of my sister's company already? Does she not please you?"

Leo sidestepped the question neatly, plastering a smile on his face. "Princess Sophia is delightful, and I enjoy spending time with her. However, it was she who suggested that if I am seen to be too attentive, false assumptions may be made about my intentions."

Stephan's brow creased, and Leo could see the moment he realised what Leo was saying. His eyes narrowed. "You truly do not intend to propose, do you?"

Leo shook his head, a minute movement. "No."

The corners of Stephan's mouth turned down. "Sometimes duty comes before preference," he said lowly. "The advantages an alliance could bring…"

"Can be explored through a trade agreement," Leo said firmly. "Your sister and I have agreed that we will not marry." Before Stephan could argue, he turned away and signalled for a glass of wine to be brought over.

He drained the glass and then linked arms with the nearest young noblewoman and put some distance between himself and the prince. When he sneaked a glance, Stephan was still frowning, but Leo ignored him.

As far as Leo was concerned, the visit had been a success. He'd avoided an unwanted betrothal without diplomatic incident, nobody's feelings had been hurt, and there were plans in place for Leo and Mattias to visit the king of Evergreen the following month to formalise the details of their new alliance which, while not quite as strong as the bond formed by a marriage, was nonetheless a satisfactory result.

Leo danced a while longer with his new partner, a willowy blonde who smiled and blushed prettily in a way that brought back fond memories of the young noblewoman he'd had a dalliance with in his late teens. It had been nice while it had lasted, but then her family had moved from Ravenport to a country estate, and he hadn't seen her again. And nowadays, rather than soft, feminine curves, he was partial to the smooth planes of a man's chest, strong thighs, and muscled buttocks that flexed and pinked under a firm hand.

If said buttocks happened to be attached to a certain smart-mouthed groom, so much the better.

Tomorrow, Leo decided, he'd reward himself for surviving this week, and go and see Felix for a ride at the first opportunity.

And afterwards, maybe they'd take the horses out.

## Chapter Eleven

Felix put his hands on his hips and arched backward, groaning with relief as the muscles of his back stretched and popped. He'd spent the morning helping Mother, the older grooms, and the stable boys make sure the visitors' horses were ready for their departure, and now he ached all over.

The tightness in his muscles didn't matter, though. What *did* matter was that when the visiting party had left the castle just before noon, every Evergreen mount had been perfectly turned out, which meant that not only was there no chance of someone taking umbrage over their horse's care, but Mother's reputation as one of the best would remain intact, something Felix knew the man valued.

"Are we done yet?" Davin whined. "We've been here for *hours*." To his credit, he'd genuinely put his back into it this morning. He had stray bits of straw in his hair, a smudge of something on one cheek, and he'd actually sweated through his clothing, which for Davin was almost unheard of. Ollie, who was standing next to him, didn't look much better, and his stomach let out a growl.

"Maybe, since they've worked so hard, the lads can have the rest of the day off," Felix suggested.

Mother hummed, the corner of his mouth quirking up as the boys shuffled from foot to foot in suppressed excitement, and Felix knew he'd guessed the head groom's intentions correctly. "I suppose you've done well enough," Mother said at last. "You're free until the evening feed, boys."

"I've heard tell that there are leftovers from the banquet last night if you go up to the kitchens," Felix added.

Ollie's eyes went wide, and his mouth dropped open. "For *us?*"

"If you're quick."

Felix let out a snort at the speed with which the two boys went scampering off towards the kitchens, and Mother shook his head fondly.

Felix stifled a yawn. He'd gotten up early to take care of Blackbird and Shadow and now he was feeling it.

Mother raised an eyebrow. "Should I give you the afternoon off as well, Flick?"

Felix shook his head. "I'm fine. There's some tack to be cleaned."

Mother put a hand on his shoulder, and it looked like he was biting back a smile. "I think you have something more important than tack to take care of right now."

Felix frowned. "What do I have to take care of?"

"*That,*" Mother said. He turned Felix so he was facing the castle yards and Felix's eyes widened when he saw the figure walking towards them. Even from this distance, Felix recognised Leo's long stride and solid build, and his heart played a staccato rhythm in his chest as his tiredness evaporated at the sight.

He'd known he missed Leo, but he hadn't realised exactly how much until right now when he could feel the smile spreading across his face.

"It looks like His Majesty wants to go riding, so I'll take care of the tack, and you take care of"—Mother gave a cough that sounded suspiciously like a laugh—"*guarding* the royal body." And with that he departed, leaving Felix alone in the stable yard.

As Leo got closer, Felix could see that there were dark smudges under his eyes, doubtless the result of too many long meetings and late nights, but there was a spring in his step which Felix took to mean that things had gone well with the visit.

Leo came to a stop in front of him, his hands curled up at his sides, and Felix didn't miss the way Leo's fingers flexed like he was fighting the urge to reach out and touch.

Felix sympathised, the need to feel those hands on his skin bubbling up in him.

He licked his lips, swallowed and said, "Your Majesty, I'm glad you're here. There's something in the stables that needs your attention."

"Oh?" Leo raised one eyebrow and smirked. "You'd better show me then."

Felix turned on his heel and led Leo into the privacy of Blackbird's box, and before he knew it he'd been backed against the wall and Leo was kissing him hot and heavy, tongue dipping into his mouth and hands roving over his shoulders and down his sides as Leo tugged at him, bringing their bodies closer.

Felix wasn't sure how long they stayed there just kissing but it was heavenly, and time became liquid and meaningless. By the time Leo pulled back, Felix was hard in his trousers, and he could feel the tell-tale bulge that meant Leo was in the same state. "Hello, sweetheart," Leo rasped out, eyes glittering darkly. "Did you miss me?"

"Of course," Felix panted. "Did you want to go to my—"

"You," Leo said, cutting him off. "I just want *you*." Leo fumbled with the fastenings on Felix's trousers and shoved them down, wrapping a broad palm around Felix's cock and jacking it in slow, sure strokes. The heat of his touch had Felix letting out a low gasp as arousal raced through him, and his hips rocked forward.

Leo gave a rough chuckle. "Impatient boy." He gave a few more firm strokes before releasing Felix's length. Felix whined at the loss but then Leo dropped to his knees and Felix's cock was engulfed in the glorious, soft heat of Leo's mouth. Felix threw his head back, his whine becoming a low groan. Leo swirled his tongue around the head of Felix's cock, his mouth moving up and down the shaft as Felix tangled a hand in Leo's hair. Leo responded by tilting his head so that Felix could thrust deeper into the warm, wet cavern of his mouth.

When Felix glanced down, Leo had his head tipped back. His eyes were dark with lust and his mouth was stretched wide around Felix's cock. The sight lit a wildfire in Felix's veins, sending heat coursing through him. Using both hands to hold Leo in place, he rocked forward, rutting into the king's mouth as his cock throbbed and his balls tightened. Leo hummed and wrapped his hands around Felix's thighs, his fingers digging into the muscle, and the exquisite sting of pleasure-pain was enough to bring Felix to completion, his whole body thrumming when he spilled down Leo's throat.

Leo didn't hesitate to swallow, and when Felix was spent he lapped gently at his softening cock until Felix shuddered and pulled away, oversensitive. He sagged against the wall for a second before sliding all the way down to the ground, his legs boneless.

Leo was still on his knees, watching him intently and looking distinctly pleased with himself. "You are a delight in the throes of passion, did you know that?" Leo said, voice hushed. "I could watch you all day."

Leo's hair was mussed, his lips were rosy and plump, and he was utterly irresistible. Leaning in and cupping Leo's face in both hands, Felix kissed him. The tang of his own spend was sharp on his tongue, strangely intimate and arousing, and Felix found himself desperate to bring Leo undone.

He rubbed the heel of his hand over the bulge in Leo's trousers and Leo groaned into his mouth. Felix pulled back, grinning, and gently shoved Leo until he was sprawled on the floor, balancing on his elbows with his legs spread wide. He wasted no time opening Leo's trousers and extracting his cock. The head was rosy and leaking, and Felix used the slippery pre-cum to slick his hand before taking a firm grip and setting up a steady rhythm. Leo grunted and spread his legs wider, his head thrown back, his mouth open and his eyes closed, and his cock hot and heavy in Felix's hand.

Leo fucked up into Felix's fist, fast and sloppy, his hips working. He let out a series of increasingly desperate noises, and Felix took pity on him and added a twist at the top of his stroke in the way he knew Leo liked. Leo let out one last choked sound and tensed before his cock pulsed with his release, leaving Felix with a warm mess in his palm and a warm glow in his chest.

Leo's entire body sagged, and he let out a low, breathless laugh. "I've missed this," he said. "I've become spoiled, bedding you."

Felix couldn't help himself. "Weren't you always spoiled, little prince?"

Leo dragged himself upright and jutted his chin out, a gleam in his eye. "Are you being *disrespectful,* boy?"

Felix raised an eyebrow in response, falling into the familiar banter. "And what are you going to do about it? *Spank* me?"

Leo grinned, sharp and provocative. "You know, I do believe I will. You'll feel the flat of my hand *and* the sting of the crop tonight."

Felix felt the tendrils of excitement curling in his gut, and his breath caught. "Y-yes, sire."

Leo's smile faltered just a little. "You sound nervous. Are you sure?"

Felix took a long, steadying breath to calm himself, then leaned in and draped his arms around Leo's neck, pressing their foreheads together. "You should know by now that I'm sure," he murmured. "That's not nerves, Leo. It's *anticipation.*"

The crease disappeared from Leo's brow, and his hungry expression returned. "Well, in that case," he said softly, "perhaps we should take the horses out today, because after I have my way with you tonight, your arse will be *far* too tender tomorrow."

Felix's cock twitched at the thought of it. "Is that a promise?"

"You know it is, brat." Leo stood and Felix followed him up, casting about for a clean rag and wiping his hand before tucking his spent cock back into his trousers. "I did mean it about riding today, though. I need to clear my head."

Felix nodded and walked out into the yard, snagging some apples on the way. He stood at the railing by the meadow and clicked his tongue, and before long Shadow and Blackbird trotted over, nostrils flaring as they sensed the presence of treats. Felix gave them their apples and led them in and saddled both horses, and before long they were off. They rode at a steady pace across the vast green plain, a soft breeze making ripples in the long grass.

The horses slowed to a walk and Felix tilted his head back, a smile on his face as he basked in the sun's rays and the presence of Leo next to him. Felix knew there could never *really* be anything between them, but still. Leo had sought him out at the first opportunity, and he couldn't help the burst of affection that ran through him. He was very fond of Leo, even if he could be a bit of a tit.

They rode in comfortable silence until they reached what Felix had started to think of as *their* grove, and Felix was overcome by a desire to hide away from the world and have Leo to himself, just for a little bit. He nodded towards the shelter of the trees. "Shall we rest?"

Leo's face lit up in a smile. "That sounds perfect."

He slid from his saddle with sinuous grace, and Felix let his eyes linger on the elegant curve of Leo's arse and the flex of his thigh muscles. He might not be able to have more, but he had *this*, so he might as well make the most of it. He dismounted his own horse and after looping both sets of reins over a tree branch, he stepped into Leo's space. He draped his body along

Leo's spine and slid his hands around his waist.

Leo hummed and turned in Felix's arms, stealing a kiss before drawing Felix down into the long grass. They lay there in the dappled sunlight trading lazy kisses, and in that moment, Felix found himself perfectly satisfied.

If all he could have was stolen moments like this, he'd take it.

He let out a contented sigh, and Leo echoed it. "It's so good to be out from under all those people watching my every move," Leo said. "Did you know I had to mind my manners for an *entire* week in case Prince Stephan took umbrage at something?"

"Imagine having to avoid offending some royal pain in the arse," Felix said drily. "I can't think what that must be like."

Leo snorted. "I'm aware of the irony of complaining about royal protocol, trust me."

"Just as long as you're aware." Felix grinned, pulling himself into a sitting position. "Did you *really* manage to behave for the week, or did Mattias spend the whole time following you around smoothing ruffled feathers?"

"Excuse you, my behavior was *exemplary*," Leo shot back. "Prince Stephan didn't even object when I told him that I had no intention of marrying his sister. That's how diplomatic I was."

"That *is* impressive, especially for you," Felix said and tried to ignore the relief flooding his veins. It wasn't like he had any claim on Leo's affections. Still, he couldn't help asking, "So you're definitely not getting married?"

Leo sat up and faced him. "Of course not. I'm perfectly happy as I am." He paused, putting one hand on Felix's thigh and squeezing lightly, fixing Felix with a steady gaze. "With you."

Felix's heart flip-flopped in his chest. It was *unfair* of Leo to say things like that when they both knew this could never be more than it was. But at the same time, Felix knew he'd hold this memory close, however this thing between them ended.

*When* it ended.

Felix swallowed the unexpected lump in his throat. He placed his hand on Leo's, removing it from his leg and standing. "I'm glad you're happy with our arrangement, sire," he said. "We should head back."

Leo's brow creased and he tensed. "What's wrong? What did I say?"

Felix swallowed again, unable to explain the bittersweet sting of knowing Leo's affection could only be temporary. "It's nothing. I'm tired, that's all. Besides, *someone* has invited me into his bed tonight and I doubt I'll be sleeping, so I was hoping to take a nap." He plastered on a smile and hoped it looked more genuine than it felt.

It must have passed muster because the tension left

Leo's shoulders and he grinned up at him and stood. "It's true. I intend to spank your arse until it's blushing harder than a virgin on her wedding night, and then pleasure you so thoroughly that you forget your own name."

Felix's smile became more genuine at that. Leo was a gifted lover, and having his full attention was like nothing Felix had ever experienced. Based on past experience, it was possible that not only would he forget his own name, he'd lose the ability to form words at all. "Well, in that case, I should definitely make sure I'm well rested."

He retrieved the horses and they mounted, taking a moment more to breathe in the sweet smell of the fresh grass before they set out. It was as they were leaving the thicket of trees that Felix paused, the hairs on the back of his neck standing up for no discernible reason. He tensed at the distant snap of a twig and held up a hand. "Did you hear that?"

"Hear what?" Leo asked, distracted with trying to rein in an unsettled Blackbird.

It was then that Felix heard another sound, and out of the corner of his eye he caught the glint of sunlight on steel. It took the barest of seconds for him to recognise that it was an arrow—and it was moving toward them at speed. His heart thundered in his chest as the realisation of what was happening hit him.

*Someone was attacking Leo.*

The arrow flew past, close enough that Felix felt the breeze of it against his cheek, and his first thought was that whoever was shooting should be sacked for such poor aim given that he wasn't even the target. His second thought was that arrows came in quivers, and he needed to get Leo to safety *now*.

Felix didn't stop to think further, his instincts and training racing to the fore as protecting Leo became his first —his *only*—concern. He leaned across and gave Blackbird's flank an almighty whack, startling the horse into a gallop as he screamed, *"Ride!"*

Leo's eyes widened before he flattened himself against Blackbird's back and took off towards the castle while urging the horse to go faster, her hooves thundering against the ground. Felix raced after him as another arrow sailed wide, followed by a third.

He could hear hooves behind them, and he leaned forward in the saddle, digging his heels into Shadow's sides and spurring the horse on as he tried to close the distance that had opened up between him and Leo. He had the short sword he always kept strapped to his belt, and he was good enough with it that he could hold his own in a fight, but he couldn't protect Leo if he wasn't close to him.

"Come *on*." He grunted through his teeth, leaning farther forward and hoping that Shadow would pick up on his urgency, and for a wonder it seemed to work. Dust flew from Shadow's hooves and the horse's sides heaved as they picked up speed, and it wasn't long before Felix was drawing level with Leo. They raced across the meadow, neck and neck.

It occurred to Felix that the last time they'd raced like this, it had been towards the stand of trees, and Felix had won. His prize had been the king's mouth around his cock, and Felix was almost certain Leo had lost on purpose.

A laugh bubbled up in Felix's chest, inappropriate and

shocked, and made its way out of his mouth. It had a hysterical edge to it, and at the sound Shadow's ears flattened against his skull. Felix sucked in a deep breath, willing himself to focus, and managed to get himself back under control as he rode forward.

But no amount of deep breathing in the world could prepare him for the solid *thwack* of an arrow hitting his saddle. He pulled on his reins reflexively, and Shadow reacted to the impact of the arrow embedding itself in the leather by rearing up onto his back legs. The next thing Felix knew, he was flying backward through the air. The ground was hard beneath him when he landed on his back, rattling every bone in his body and knocking the wind out of him.

Pain flared through him and jarred up his spine where he'd hit the dirt, and for a few seconds he was paralyzed, unable to even draw a breath, before a strange croaking sound came out of his mouth, and he gasped in precious air.

Shadow's hooves were far too close for his liking, so he rolled over to lessen his chances of being trampled, which proved to be a mistake. His vision greyed out for a moment as a wave of pain flared from his side and he struggled not to be sick. He closed his eyes and breathed in and out, slow and steady, trying to ignore the way every breath brought a fresh stab of hurt.

Someone was touching him, cradling his head and calling his name with increasing panic. "Felix? Felix? *Flick?* Oh gods, are you all right?"

He opened his eyes to find Leo crouched in front of him, his face twisted in concern. "Are you all right?" he repeated, his voice taking on a desperate note. His hands darted about as he petted uselessly at Felix's shirt, like he wanted to help but didn't quite know how, and all Felix could think was *why aren't you running?*

He dragged himself into a sitting position, wincing at the ache in his arse and his side, and gasped out, "What the *fuck* are you still doing here?"

Leo reared back like he'd been slapped. "You're *hurt.*"

"And you're the *king*. It's my job to keep you safe." Felix breathed through another burst of pain and hoped he hadn't cracked a rib.

"But you're *hurt,*" Leo repeated. "I can't leave you." His bottom lip quivered, and Felix didn't know whether to kiss him for his concern or slap him for his stupidity.

Given the situation, he bypassed the kissing and barked out, "Oh, for the love of giblets, will you stop being so stupid and *get on your damn horse?* I'm fine! Just bruised, not broken. I'll be along in a minute." He followed it up with the sternest glare he could muster.

Leo opened his mouth, caught the look Felix was giving him, and closed it again. He mounted his horse and galloped off.

It was a relief when he was gone because it meant Felix could finally stop pretending that he didn't hurt all over. He slumped back onto the ground, lying as still as he could manage, and waited for their attackers to catch up to him and either put him out of his misery or add to it.

Except, after several long minutes, there seemed to be a distinct lack of murderous figures anywhere nearby. Felix levered himself upright again and, shading his eyes with his hand, peered back the way they'd come, still expecting assassins on horseback to come racing towards him. But there was nobody there.

Whoever had been after them—after *Leo*, because nobody was interested in the son of a guard—had obviously fled once they'd failed. They'd probably be back, but for now at least, Felix had done his job.

He'd saved Leo's life.

He stifled a hysterical giggle at the thought that he'd *actually* guarded Leo's body for a change, before dragging himself to standing. With a lot of cursing, he snagged Shadow's reins and managed to haul himself up into the saddle. The sharp ache in his ribs and arse had lessened to a dull thud, and he was able to slump across Shadow's back and slowly, slowly make his way back to the stable yard. He passed a dozen guards thundering the other way on horseback, so he assumed Leo had made it back, and the tension in his gut eased at the knowledge that the king was safe.

Shadow walked at a gentle, easy pace, as though sensing his condition, and when he got back to the stables he found his father waiting for him, white-faced and thin-lipped.

"Gods, son, are you all right?" Janus hurried over and held out his arms, and the sight of his father there waiting to catch him, just like he had been Felix's entire life, was enough for Felix to let go of the last shred of stubbornness that had been keeping him upright. He slid from the saddle and into his father's hold, let out a mumbled "Ow," as the pain in his side flared, and promptly passed out.

## Chapter Twelve

Leo *rode.*
He rode like the devils of hell were after him—which, in a way, they were. Someone was trying to kill him, and if it wasn't for Felix and his quick thinking, they might well have succeeded.

His heart was thundering like it wanted to escape his chest, and he wasn't sure if it was from the attempt on his life or from the sight of Felix lying sprawled in the dirt, gasping for breath. Both were equally horrifying. He'd seen Felix topple from his horse, and Leo's blood had run cold for a split second when he'd thought Felix had taken an arrow. The relief he'd felt when it became clear that Felix had simply been thrown had been overwhelming.

He'd wanted nothing more than to stay and help Felix up, but even though he was clearly injured, Felix had reminded Leo in no uncertain terms that his primary responsibility was to his kingdom. The glare he'd sent Leo's way had convinced him that the boy couldn't be too badly injured, not if he could manage a scowl of that magnitude.

So now here he was, riding away from his lover and desperately wishing he wasn't. He didn't turn around, though—he wasn't a fool. Instead, he galloped like a wild thing, urging Blackbird on until the stable yard came into view.

"*Send for the guard!*" he called as he clattered over the cobbles and Blackbird tossed her mane and snorted, picking up on his distress.

Mother Jones appeared, and his mouth dropped open. "Your Majesty?"

Leo managed to settle Blackbird enough that he could dismount and hand the reins off. "Someone tried to kill me!" he gasped out, and somehow, saying it aloud made it real in a way it hadn't been before.

He had to stop for a moment, setting his hands on his knees and bending over, his breathing suddenly shaky. "Someone tried to *kill* me," he whispered, and for all the times he and Mattias had joked about assassination attempts, it really wasn't very funny at all. He stumbled into the stables and sat heavily on a low stool.

Mother looped the reins around a post and crouched in front of Leo. "Are you injured, Your Majesty?" he asked, low and urgent.

Leo flapped a hand. "No. Whoever was firing the arrows was a terrible shot." He swallowed. "Felix was hurt, though." Mother's eyes widened. "Not by the archers," Leo hastened to add. "His horse threw him. I wanted to stay and help, but he yelled at me and called me stupid. He insisted he'd be fine and that I should leave him." Leo hoped Mother didn't notice the way his voice hitched.

"Begging your pardon, sire, he was right to do so,"

Mother said gently. "Now let's get you safely up to the castle and then we'll send the guards out."

"I want to wait for Felix—"

"If Flick was well enough to shout at you, he can't be too badly hurt. He's probably just bruised."

"That's what he said," Leo muttered. "Bruised, not broken."

"There you go then." A hand gripped his elbow and Mother drew him to his feet. "I'm sorry, but it's not safe for you here."

Just then there was the sound of multiple boots running across the courtyard and Mattias skidded into view, followed by the captain of the guard and ten or so men with their weapons drawn.

"Leo?" Mattias gasped out. "One of the guards saw you from the window, said you were fairly flying back towards the stables. What happened?"

"Someone tried to kill His Majesty!" Mother said.

Mattias's eyes went wide before his mouth pressed into a thin line and a deep crease appeared between his brows. "Tell me what happened."

Leo swallowed. "Someone was firing arrows at me out near our—near that stand of trees with the little stream where the horses like to graze. Felix saved me."

Mattias blew out a long breath and his shoulders hunched up tight. Then he was dragging Leo in close and hugging him so tightly he couldn't breathe. "Don't you *dare* get killed, you hear me?" he rasped in Leo's ear, and Leo wondered how it was that someone caring about him somehow managed to make him feel better and worse all at once.

His eyes grew hot and his composure, such as it was, came dangerously close to faltering, but just this once, Leo didn't care about appearances and let his head rest against Mattias's chest, the heartbeat under his ear steady and reassuring. "They missed," he mumbled into Mattias's shirt, blinking the dampness away. "Whoever hired them should get their money back."

Mattias pulled back and tilted his head. "Where's Felix?"

Leo swallowed around the sudden lump in his throat. "Felix is—" He found he couldn't bring himself to tell Mattias that Felix had been hurt.

Thankfully, he didn't have to. "Young Flick took a tumble off his mount, sir," Mother said, "but His Majesty tells me that he's making his way back. He insisted the king get to safety first."

Mattias looked to Leo, who nodded. "Shadow threw him, but he told me he was only bruised and to go ahead without him. Frankly, him shouting at me was more terrifying than the thought of the assassins."

From where he'd been standing, Janus breathed a shaky sigh and his shoulders sagged.

Mattias addressed the guards. "I want you to ride out and see who or what you can find. Not you, Janus," he added. "You stay here and wait for your boy."

"Thank you, sir," Felix's father said, his brow creased with worry, and Leo felt a pang of sympathy for him through his own shock.

The rest of the guards hurried over to the main stables and Mattias turned to Mother. "Mr. Jones, can you take care of Blackbird? I'm taking His Majesty to safety."

And with that, Mattias wrapped an arm around Leo's shoulders and led him back towards the castle. Behind them, Leo could hear the guards mounting up and preparing to ride.

"I can't believe someone *actually* tried to kill me," he said, the reality of it hitting him all over again.

Mattias shrugged. "I can. You're incredibly annoying."

It was, oddly enough, exactly what he needed to hear, and he wrapped an arm around Mattias's waist in silent thanks as they made their way across the cobbles.

"And you're *sure* you didn't get a look at them, sire?"

"*No,*" Leo insisted for what felt like the thousandth time. "The first I knew of it was Felix setting Blackbird off in a gallop and telling me to ride. It was only when I looked back that I saw the arrows flying. It all happened so quickly, I didn't see where they came from."

The members of the Royal Council were seated around a long table in the main chambers, and one of them looked like he was about to speak again, but Mattias cut in. "I think we've established that His Majesty has told us all he can."

There was a tap on the door and Mattias strode over and opened it to reveal Janus Hobson standing there, face drawn. Leo's heart stuttered in his chest, and he had to hold back the urge to grab the man by his lapels and demand to know if Felix was all right.

It turned out there was no need. Janus turned to Leo

and gave a tired smile. "I thought you'd like to know, sire. Felix made it back safely. A party of guards has scoured the area and found no evidence of the would-be assassins, so we suspect it was just a stray malcontent, but nonetheless we'll be stepping up your security until Felix is able to resume his duties."

All Leo's breath left him in a rush. "Thank you," he said, bowing his head slightly.

Mattias resumed his place next to Leo at the head of the long oak table and addressed the council. "I don't think there's anything to be gained by discussing this further."

"Quite," Leo agreed, standing. "Captain Hobson, a word in private if you please?" He turned his back on the council members just in case they hadn't quite gotten the hint that he was done with them, and it was only a matter of moments before he heard chair legs scraping against the stone floor and the shuffle of feet. The men trailed out, bowing their heads as they passed, until Leo was left alone with Mattias and Janus.

"How is he really?" Leo asked at once. "Is he all right?"

Janus grimaced. "He's black and blue all up one side, but the physician tells me that's the worst of it, and a few days of rest should see him right as rain."

The tension Leo had been carrying in his muscles melted away at hearing the news, and his shoulders slumped. "Excellent. Is he still here? You *did* take him to the castle physician and not to some sawbones in the town, right?"

Janus raised an eyebrow. "Well, since he was injured protecting *you*, I assumed you'd want him to have the best care possible. Or would you have preferred me to load him into a cart while he was unconscious and take him down to the village, *sire?*"

Well, that answered any questions Leo might have had as to where Felix got his attitude from.

He found that right at this moment, he didn't care much about etiquette, more interested in Felix's recovery. "Actually, I was going to suggest Felix stay at the castle while he recuperates," he said. "His cottage is too—"

Mattias cleared his throat.

"—far away from the physician's office if he needs medical attention," Leo said smoothly. "We don't want him to have to walk all that way."

Janus nodded, face carefully blank. "He's still with the physician, having arnica cream applied. I'll let him know."

"I'll tell him myself," Leo said. "I want to see him and check he's all right."

And perhaps steal a kiss to make himself feel better, but there was no need to mention that.

"I'll escort you to the infirmary, sire," Janus said.

"I know the way," Leo said and made to walk towards the door, only to be stopped in his tracks by both Mattias and Janus stepping in front of him, blocking his path.

"Sorry, but you don't go anywhere alone, at least for now," Mattias said.

Leo pouted. "Surely I'm safe in my own castle?"

"It would be foolish to wander about unprotected," Janus said, folding his arms over his chest in a move that was reminiscent of Felix when he had his dander up about something.

Mattias put a hand on Leo's shoulder. "Let the man do his job, Leo. You hired him because he's the best, after all."

Leo sighed. An escort wasn't the worst idea he'd heard. It was just going to take some getting used to, that was all. The castle was the one place he'd always felt free to move about at will.

He guessed he wouldn't be making any midnight visits to see Felix. Still, he could visit him *now*, and that was something. He squared his shoulders and said, "I'm grateful for your protection, Captain. If you wouldn't mind escorting me to the infirmary, I'd like to thank your son personally."

"I'm not sure he's well enough for a vigorous…thanking," Janus said, almost completely straight-faced.

No, Felix's irreverent apple hadn't fallen far from the family tree at all, had it?

Still, Leo had to admire the way Janus toed the edges of the line skirting disrespect. He did it so skilfully that you could barely see where the chalk had been scuffed.

"I'll make sure my thanks are suitably restrained," Leo said, and didn't bother to hide his relieved smile as they walked down the staircase and along the long stone corridors into the far reaches of the castle where the physician's rooms were situated.

Leo knocked on the door and didn't wait for a reply before walking in while Janus waited outside. He was met with the sight of Felix, naked and facedown on the physician's table, and Leo couldn't help the gasp that left him. Felix's left side was a riot of colour, reds and blues that would turn purple soon enough. There was one bruise in particular that covered most of an arse cheek, but he looked otherwise unharmed.

The physician, a small man with thinning hair who was

just putting the lid back on a jar of salve, barked out, "*What?* You can't just barge—" His mouth snapped shut when he turned and saw Leo. "*Your Majesty!*" His cheeks turned red as he fumbled and threw a blanket over Felix's lower half. "Deepest apologies, sire, I didn't know it was you!" He swallowed and gave a hasty half bow, hands clenching reflexively at his sides.

Leo felt some sympathy for the man—after all, he *had* just barged in. "It's fine, Maester Owens," he said. "I just wanted to check on my guard."

Felix turned his head. "Majesty?"

Leo was at his bedside in an instant, and it took all his restraint not to run a hand down the curve of Felix's spine or lean in and kiss the top of his head. He gripped the side of the table to keep his instincts in check and said, "Felix. I wanted to come and check on you. Is the physician taking good care of you?"

"Yes, sire." Felix propped himself up on his elbows, pulling a face and moving slowly. "Nothing's broken. It's just bruising."

"Good, good," Leo said and wondered what to say next. He *wanted* to tell Felix off for putting himself in danger, and he *wanted* to make him promise he wouldn't do it again, but that wasn't appropriate to say to someone whose job was to put themselves at risk, was it? And it *certainly* wasn't done for a king to tell his supposedly casual lover that he'd been terrified at the thought of losing him. He settled for saying, "I'm glad you weren't badly injured."

"I'm glad I wasn't badly injured as well, sire," Felix said, and the soft smile he gave Leo said he'd heard what Leo wasn't saying.

"I've arranged for you to recover at the castle, where I—I mean, where *the maester* can look after you."

"Thank you, sire," Felix said. "He's taken excellent care of me so far."

The physician puffed out his chest. "We'll have him up and about in no time."

"You have my appreciation," Leo said, and the man beamed. Leo tried to think of a subtle way to get the man out of the room, but he was too rattled to find an excuse, so in the end he just said, "Would you mind if I asked you to step out, Maester? I wish to have a private conversation with my guard."

"Of course, Your Majesty. Shall I come back in...an hour?"

"That will be fine," Leo said and waited for the man to leave.

The maester fluttered about for a moment, wiping his hands and straightening Felix's blanket, and it took all of Leo's patience not to push him towards the door, but finally he gave a small bow and left, and they were alone.

As soon as he heard the click of the door closing, Leo was bending over the bed, pressing kisses to the back of Felix's neck and running a hand down the length of his spine like he'd wanted to do since he'd arrived, desperate to reassure himself that Felix really was here and safe and whole.

"You could have been killed," he whispered against Felix's skin. "I was *so* worried." His hand encountered the edge of the blanket and he eased it down, pulling back so he could see Felix's injuries properly. "Oh, sweetheart." He said with a sigh, his chest growing tight. He ghosted his fingertips over the massive purpling bruise on Felix's arse and gave in to the impulse to lean down and kiss it.

The skin was greasy with salve and warm under his lips, and Leo didn't care. He did it again and again, peppering the area with soft pecks until Felix laughed and said, "I thought only the king got his arse kissed by an angel?"

"Hush, you," Leo mumbled, but he pulled back. "How badly does it hurt? Be honest."

Felix eased himself onto one side and winced as he swung his legs over the side of the table and sat up with careful movements. He wrapped his arms around Leo's neck and pressed their foreheads together. "It throbs, mainly," he said. "But I've had worse. I'm more concerned that someone wants you dead." His grip tightened, and it struck Leo that perhaps Felix was as worried for him as he'd been for Felix.

There was no denying the warm glow that spread through Leo at the thought that Felix *cared*, but he set it aside for now in favour of providing what reassurances he could. "It's fine. The guards scoured the area and didn't find anything. They think it was just a random attack."

"Still." Felix buried his face into the curve of Leo's throat, his voice muffled. "I don't like the idea of you being in danger."

"Well, it's not exactly my favourite thing either, but it goes with the territory, sweetheart. And I feel better knowing I have you there protecting me." Leo wrapped his arms around Felix's back, careful to keep his touch gentle.

"I'll always be there," Felix murmured, his breath warm on Leo's skin, and Leo had to close his eyes against the sudden sting there.

Because Felix obviously meant he'd be there as Leo's *bodyguard*, but Leo realised with an awful, sinking certainty that he wanted so much more. He wanted Felix as his lover, permanently.

And what he wanted, he couldn't ever have.

## Chapter Thirteen

Felix stared at the ceiling and sighed.

He was *bored*. He'd been confined to the infirmary for eight entire days. It was longer than he'd ever rested in his *life*, and it was torture. His skin itched with the need to be up and about, but the physician was firm. He'd declared that the king had insisted Felix should be on bed rest, and so on bed rest he would remain.

True, he wasn't completely healed, but his bruises only ached now, and Felix couldn't shake the feeling that he was malingering. Part of it, he knew, was worrying about who was taking care of Leo.

Leo, who he'd only seen three times in eight days in brief, strained visits under the watchful eye of the king's now-constant guard.

And Felix understood, he did. Now that Leo was under continuous supervision, it wasn't like he could slip along to the infirmary at will, not without someone wondering why the king was so concerned with the health of someone who was, after all, just one of the castle staff. Appreciation for

Felix saving his life could only explain a certain level of attention. Still, Felix couldn't help but think that the hours would have passed much faster with Leo for company.

Not that he'd been alone, exactly. Maester Owens checked on him *far* more often than Felix felt was necessary, especially after he'd caught Felix trying to sneak out on his second day there.

He'd had almost daily visits from his mother, naturally, and he'd welcomed her presence as she fussed over him in a way that made him feel small and safe all at once. She'd arrived at the castle the day he'd been hurt, sweeping aside the physician's assertions that Felix was resting, and sailed into his room bringing cake and cheek kisses and comfort. She'd clicked her tongue over his injuries and made loud noises about how she hoped the king appreciated that all the men in her life insisted on putting themselves in danger on his behalf.

Felix had been quick to assure her that Leo was *most* appreciative, memories of warm lips against the bruised skin of his arse springing to mind.

His father had also been to see him daily, and although Felix had quizzed him at length about the possible identity of the assassin, it seemed that the attempt really had been a one-time thing, with no sign of the attacker and no further attempts on Leo's life.

Felix had been more relieved at hearing that than he'd wanted to admit.

Mother Jones popped in to see him regularly, telling him they missed him and keeping him updated on the health of the horses. On one occasion he made Felix laugh until his sides ached, telling him about how Davin had spent an afternoon doubled over, clutching his stomach and wailing to anyone who would listen that he was dying from colic, a term he'd doubtless heard in the stables. It had turned out to be a bellyache from stealing an apple pie from the kitchen and consuming the entire thing in one sitting.

And Felix appreciated all those visits, truly he did…but he missed *Leo*.

After the previous week when they'd barely seen each other, he'd thought that once the foreign contingent left, they'd be able to spend some time together. But of course, that had all gone to hell with the assassination attempt.

The thought of it still made Felix sick to his stomach, and it wasn't helped by lying in bed, turning the whole thing over in his mind and considering all the ways it could have ended badly.

If he hadn't spotted the arrow in time…if Blackbird had been slower to run…if the archer had had better aim… Felix shuddered when he thought about what might have happened, which in turn made him far too aware of the depths of his affection for Leo.

It was meant to be a *fling*.

He sighed again and got off the bed and lifted his shirt, checking the state of his side in the mirror. His bruising had faded to a mottled green-yellow, and he decided in a fit of rebellion that he'd *insist* that he be allowed to leave today. Being cooped up inside was giving him far too much time to think, and he was desperate for fresh air and sunshine and the distraction of hard work.

As he glared at his patchwork skin, willing it to heal

faster, there was a tap at the door and a moment later it opened a crack to reveal Leo peering in. "Felix?"

"Leo!" Despite himself, Felix felt his face split into a grin.

Leo slipped into the room, eyes sparkling, and closed the door behind himself and locked it. He hurried over to where Felix was standing. His hands tangled in the fabric of Felix's shirt and he pulled him close and kissed him. Felix closed his eyes and savoured it, soaking in Leo's touch like it was the first cool rains after the heat of summer, and Felix was parched earth.

"Missed you. Missed *this*," Leo growled under his breath.

"Mmm," Felix agreed, kissing back, his tongue probing Leo's mouth as he explored him anew, testing to make sure everything was just as he remembered.

He would have happily stayed there kissing, but he couldn't help the pained squeak when Leo gripped his bruised hip slightly too hard.

Leo let go like he'd been scalded, eyes going wide. "Oh gods, did I hurt you?"

Felix sighed. "It's a bruise, Leo. I've had worse from the crop."

"That's different," Leo insisted. "That's *fun*." He prodded Felix's chest. "Shouldn't you be in bed? I distinctly remember ordering bed rest. And why isn't someone here watching you?"

Felix fought and lost the battle to keep from rolling his eyes. Perhaps it was a good thing Leo hadn't been visiting if he was going to fuss like this. "I *was* resting, until you turned up. And anyway, aren't *you* the one meant to be under guard?"

"Mattias is watching me. He's outside. I confess that I'd hoped we'd have the opportunity for a little…" Leo sighed. "Never mind. You're still injured. Back to bed."

Leo placed his hands at Felix's waist and tried to back him towards the four-poster, but after being confined to one room for so long, Felix was done with being bossed about like a child, and he stood firm. "Actually, I was planning on telling the maester I'm recovered and that I'd like to leave today."

Leo tilted his chin back and folded his arms across his chest. "You most certainly are not!"

Felix widened his stance and folded his own arms across his chest, looking Leo in the eye. "I'm *fine*. Normal people who *aren't* kings manage to do their jobs with cuts and scrapes and bruises all the time."

He held Leo's gaze until Leo sighed and dropped his head. "Am I being an idiot about this?"

"Normally, if you have to ask that question, the answer's yes." Felix gave a wry grin to let Leo know he didn't mind him showing concern, not really.

Leo's head jerked up. "Rude!"

Felix shrugged. "I thought you liked it when I gave you cheek, because it means you have an excuse to colour *my* cheeks."

The concern faded from Leo's eyes and the smile he gave was dark and full of promise and *far* preferable to his fussing. "Brat. I can't *wait* till you're back in full health so I can spank you properly. I have a brand-new brush, and it's not for use on my hair."

Felix stepped close and slid his hands down Leo's back, feeling the breadth of the muscles there, and a shiver ran through him as he imagined them flexing while Leo spanked him. He placed a series of soft kisses up the side of Leo's throat, and Leo tilted his head back and let out a shaky moan when Felix scraped his teeth over the tendons of his throat. "If the maester says I'm well enough to go back to my cottage, does that mean I'm well enough to come and see you tonight?" Felix murmured, fairly certain he already knew the answer.

To his surprise, Leo hesitated. "About that."

Felix stepped back, his stomach twisting with nerves. Had Leo come to tell him that this was over, that he was tired of him already?

Leo must have read the worry on his face because he said, "I'd like nothing better than to see you tonight, but Princess Sophia is arriving back this afternoon for a week's stay. I'm not sure if I'll be free."

It was so unexpected that Felix pulled up short. "What?" Why was Sophia coming back? Unless... "Don't tell me she's decided to marry you after all?" he asked, dreading the answer.

Leo actually laughed, and the knots in Felix's stomach unravelled slightly. His tension eased further when Leo said, "In truth, she's sweet on one of my knights, and while this trip is dressed up as trade talks, I suspect she's here to woo her man. So at least I'm safe from the spectre of matrimony."

Felix should have been comforted, but his heart dropped as he was hit by the hopelessness of the situation. Leo might not marry Sophia, but he'd marry *someone*—and it wouldn't be Felix. "Safe for now," he said quietly.

Leo gave him a sharp look. "I beg your pardon?"

Felix took a deep breath. "For now. You *will* have to marry and provide an heir eventually. It's almost a shame it's not Sophia, because I think you could actually be happy together."

"Oh, absolutely not," Leo said. "She's far too clever for me and would likely murder me in my sleep for my annoying habits. And anyway, why are you suddenly so keen on marrying me off?" His brow creased.

"I'm not. I'm just being realistic. This"—Felix waved a hand between them and swallowed hard—"is fun, but we both know it doesn't—*can't*—mean anything." His chest constricted at the lie.

Leo took a half step back like he'd been struck, and his mouth opened then closed again before he said, "Flick, you must know that's not true. I'm very fond of you. In fact, not seeing you these last few weeks has shown me just *how* fond. I think I might—"

"*Don't.*" Felix forced the word out before Leo said something they'd both regret. "Don't say what I think you're about to say, because I can't say it back."

The look Leo gave him was nothing short of betrayed. "Are you saying you don't care?"

"I'm saying I know how this goes. Maybe you won't marry this princess, or even the next one, but it's bound to be one of them. Sooner or later, you'll end up wed and bred with some pretty young thing, doing your duty for the kingdom." Felix's eyes burned and he turned away so Leo wouldn't see.

"And what if I don't? What if I just let the throne pass to my cousin?" There was a note of pleading in Leo's voice that almost had Felix turning back. Just for a moment, a shard of something that felt suspiciously like hope pierced his heart. It was sharper than any blade he'd ever encountered—and more deadly too, because he knew even as he felt it that it was false. He also knew that if he entertained the hope those words awoke in him for even a moment, he'd end up with his heart sliced to ribbons.

"Your cousin's not fit to walk a dog, let alone run a kingdom. He's known as Evan the Embarrassment. You can't tell me you'd seriously consider letting him inherit the throne."

Leo's silence told him all he needed to know.

"That's what I thought." Even though he'd been expecting it, the tacit rejection stung. Felix let out a shaky breath, squared his shoulders, and pretended that he wasn't hurting inside. "I'm going for a ride. I need to clear my head."

"Don't leave. Please."

Felix forced himself not to turn around. "I'll be careful," he said, deliberately misunderstanding. "I won't take Shadow past a walk." He sat on the edge of the bed and pulled his boots on, keeping his head down.

"Will you come to me tonight?" Leo's voice was barely a whisper. "Just to talk?"

Felix wasn't sure what there was left to talk about. Still, he found himself saying, "Of course."

Even now, as much as his heart ached, he found he couldn't say no to the man he was almost certainly in love with.

Shadow's coat was warm, his body was solid enough for Felix to lean against comfortably, and the horse didn't judge him as, his face buried deep in horsehair, he sniffed through a few stupid tears that he couldn't quite hold back.

Felix didn't allow himself to fall apart for long, though. It wasn't like he had anything to fall apart *about,* he reminded himself. There had been a conversation, that was all. And he'd been the one who'd been stupid enough to start it, instead of just leaving well enough alone. But nothing had really changed between them, and nothing *had* to change between them—as long as Felix was careful never to mention anything about princesses or marriage or feelings ever again.

He wiped his eyes on his sleeve and saddled Shadow, tensing at the last lingering ache as he mounted. As soon as he was seated, he felt peace flowing through his veins, so he considered the throb in his arse worth it—just like after a good fucking.

Maybe a good fucking was what he needed, he mused as he walked Shadow gently out along the trail that ran though the meadow. Maybe what he thought was emotion was just frustration, and a decent orgasm would take the edge off.

He *would* go and see Leo tonight, and he'd let Leo fuss over all his tender spots, and then they'd make some variety of love. Afterwards he might even stay the night, just to let Leo know that things were fine between them, and with any luck, Leo would forget they were meant to be talking at all.

Decision made, Felix turned his attention to enjoying his ride. Shadow ambled along the path, taking advantage of the slower pace to nibble at the shrubs they passed. Felix let himself slouch and be carried along, reins loose between his fingertips as he tipped his head back and soaked up the sun on his face and savoured the soft tendrils of breeze that played around the base of his neck.

By the time he'd ridden out past the grove, his muscles ached from the unaccustomed exercise, and there were the lingering remnants of discomfort from his injuries, but he ignored them. For the first time in eight days, he was outside, alone, and truly relaxed. Being able to close his eyes and lose himself in thought as Shadow ambled along was a balm to his soul, and he felt peace settle over him.

Which was why the blow to the back of his skull came as such a shock.

## Chapter Fourteen

Leo wanted nothing more than to chase after Felix, take him in his arms, and promise him the world, but he wasn't a fool. Felix was right, and Leo *hated* that he was right. But the fact remained that the day was coming when Leo would need to produce an heir, and Leo would struggle to find someone willing to bear his child while still allowing him to carry on a relationship with his groom.

Because what they had *was* a relationship.

Leo hadn't intended it to be anything more than a mutually satisfying arrangement, truly. But Felix, with his irreverent attitude, quick wit, clever mind, and easy smile, had somehow become so much more than a dalliance, and now Leo found his thoughts filled with the boy.

Giving him up was unthinkable.

A lump in his throat made it hard to swallow as he took in the empty bed and the empty room, but he breathed slow and deep until he had some semblance of control.

If he was honest, the pragmatic part of him was *glad*

that Felix had stopped him before he'd said something stupid. Confessing his feelings would only have destroyed any chance of them carrying on as they were. And maybe it was selfish, but if what they had now was all Leo could have, he'd take it, even if that meant pretending that what happened between them was nothing more than fun and fuckery.

Now wasn't the time to get emotional. Leo shouldn't even have been here in the first place. He should have been preparing for Sophia's visit. But he'd missed Felix fiercely, and, knowing the next few days would be far too busy for any kind of meaningful contact, had whined and wheedled at Mattias for *"just a quarter hour visit, Matty, it's been days,"* until Mattias had rolled his eyes and given in.

There was a knock on the door and Mattias poked his head inside. "I saw Flick leaving. Is everything all right?"

Leo forced a smile onto his face. "Everything's fine. He assures me he's recovered and he's desperate for fresh air, so he's decided to go riding."

Mattias raised one eyebrow in silent disbelief. Leo didn't rise to the bait, unwilling to share the details of their conversation while the hurt still felt so raw. Instead, he ran a hand through his hair, huffed out a breath and, in a blatant attempt to change the subject, said, "When are we expecting the princess?"

Something in Leo's expression must have told Mattias to leave well enough alone, because he didn't pursue the matter and instead said, "Within the hour. You'll be spending the afternoon with her going over some of those border territories that King Andros would like to acquire."

The land in question had a topography that made it

impractical for anyone who wasn't three-fourths mountain goat to live there, but the soil was rich and fertile and it would make excellent farmland, which was why the king of Evergreen was keen to claim it.

"You're joining us, of course?"

"Of course." Mattias rapped his knuckles against the door frame. "Come on. We have time to go over the details one more time before the entourage arrives."

"Right. Of course." Leo strode out of the room and followed Mattias to his offices, all the while reminding himself that now wasn't the time to worry about whether Felix was upset with him. He had a kingdom to rule and a treaty to broker.

It was just that right now, neither of those things seemed very important.

∽

The princess arrived with a much smaller entourage than previously—only one lady's maid and half a dozen guards—and there was a lot less pomp and ceremony surrounding this visit. Leo was glad of it. Even though the attempt on his life hadn't been repeated, he wasn't sure he wanted to welcome dozens of strangers into his court.

He had no such qualms about Sophia, however. She'd proved herself trustworthy by keeping her knowledge of his affair with Felix quiet. She would have been quite within her rights to depart in a flurry of scandal and demand the land she wanted as reparation for the insult to her character. Instead, she'd kept her peace, and for that Leo was eternally grateful.

He greeted her warmly, and once the pleasantries were out of the way and she'd partaken of a light luncheon and refreshed herself, they met in his office. Along with Mattias, they pored over maps of the territory in question as they entered the first stages of negotiation.

But Leo found himself unable to concentrate, his mind circling back to Felix. Would he keep his word and come to Leo's rooms tonight? Or would he think better of it?

Leo wouldn't blame him if he decided not to come, not after the way they'd left things. But it still hurt to even think of Felix rejecting him, and when Leo replayed their conversation over in his head, he wasn't sure which part of it he regretted more—the bit where he'd implied he'd let his cousin inherit the throne, or the part where he'd failed to stand by his offer.

He found himself glancing out of the window far more often than he ought to, straining for a glimpse of a familiar figure on horseback just so he'd know Felix was back safe.

He felt a pang of envy at the thought of Felix out riding Shadow. Mattias and Janus had both told him in no uncertain terms that there would be no riding for him until the spies they'd sent out had returned and they knew more about the identity of his attacker. Leo wouldn't dream of going against them, but he missed the feeling of a mount under him more than he'd thought he would. Combined with his inability to spend any time with Felix, it was no wonder he was out of sorts when he'd been denied two of his favourite things.

"Your Majesty?" Sophia's voice broke through his

thoughts and Leo realised he'd been staring out the window again for the fourth or possibly fifth time since they'd started the meeting.

"Apologies," he said and went to turn his attention back to the map, but Sophia pulled it out from under his hand and rolled it up, and then had the audacity to tap him on the shoulder with it.

"Sit," she commanded.

Leo sat.

She gave a small, satisfied nod and turned to Mattias. "Chancellor, clear the room. His Majesty and I have some things to discuss. You'll stay, of course," she added when Mattias hesitated.

Mattias dismissed the guards, and when it was just the three of them, Sophia put a hand on one hip and with the other tapped the desk with the map. "What's going on, Leopold? Why is your head in the clouds?"

"My head is *not* in the clouds," Leo said in protest. It was true—it was in the stables.

"No? Then why did you just let me talk you out of an extra five miles of territory?"

"Did I?" Leo blinked.

"Yes. Thank goodness your chancellor has a decent brain in his head, or I could have reduced your kingdom to the city of Ravenport by now without you noticing." Her eyes narrowed. "Is it something to do with your pretty groom?"

"No," Leo lied. "I'm still unsettled by the attempt on my life, if you must know." It was the best he could manage at short notice.

"Yes, I heard about that." She took a seat opposite him

at the table, elbows resting in a most unladylike manner as she leaned forward and held his gaze. "But I don't think that's it, unless you keep looking out the window for your attacker. So, I can only conclude that your attention is fixed on your young man."

Mattias had the audacity to let out a low chuckle. "Well spotted, ma'am."

Sophia turned a brilliant smile on him. "Since Leopold seems to be struck dumb, perhaps you can enlighten me as to why I'm wasting my time here while he moons and stares out the window?"

"I'm not struck dumb," Leopold said. "It's just—" He sighed.

Sophia's expression softened. "Has he left you?"

Leo hesitated. He considered telling the princess that it was none of her business, but her gaze was warm, and she seemed like she might just understand. He sighed again, deeper this time. "I...don't think so? But we have had something of a falling out."

"I knew it," Mattias said. "When Felix left, he had a face like a kicked puppy."

Sophia sat back in her chair, set the map down, and folded her hands in her lap. "And where is he now?"

"Riding," Leo muttered. "He said he needed to clear his head."

"And you didn't go after him and apologise for whatever stupid thing you said?"

"Why are you assuming I'm the one who said something stupid?" Leo crossed his arms over his chest defensively.

Mattias and Sophia exchanged a look before Mattias said, "Experience?"

"I could have you stripped of your knighthood, you know," Leo grumbled.

Mattias didn't even have the good grace to look concerned, instead flapping a dismissive hand. "If you were going to do it, you would have done it years ago."

Sophia let out a snorting laugh. "I do love that you keep him humble," she said to Mattias, giving him another dazzling smile before turning her attention back to Leo. "I find myself in need of fresh air. I'm going to go and walk in the castle gardens, and *you're* going to go to the stables and see your groom."

"He might not be back yet," Leo said, even as something that was either excitement or foreboding fluttered in his chest.

"Well, if he isn't, you'll wait there and work on your apology, won't you?" Sophia said, standing. She extended an arm to Mattias and dipped her head. "Chancellor, would you do me the courtesy of accompanying me on my walk?"

Mattias's eyes lit up, and he gave a bright smile. "I'd be glad to, ma'am."

"Please, call me Sophia." She returned the smile and linked arms with Mattias and the two of them departed, leaving Leo alone with his rolled-up map and too-fast beating heart.

He sat frozen for a moment, and then he was up and walking out the door. Janus, who'd been keeping watch outside the offices, fell into step alongside him as he strode down the corridors and headed for the stables, and Leo accepted his presence without comment.

Together the two men made their way across the courtyard, boots ringing out a quick rhythm against the cobbles. Leo was so sure that Felix would be waiting for him that when he got to the stables and the only person there was Mother Jones, the weight of his disappointment made it hard to breathe for a moment.

"Your Majesty?" Mother said, pausing in his brushing of Blackbird's mane. "Are you riding today?"

Leo swallowed past his dismay. "Not today, no," he said. "I was hoping Felix was here, actually."

Mother tilted his head at the empty stall. "I haven't seen him. Shadow's gone, so I assumed he must be riding."

Leo frowned. "Still? Shouldn't he be back by now? He's been gone for hours."

"Has he? Apologies, Your Majesty, but I didn't see him leave. I was out trying to find Davin. The little bugger skived off again, and he's taken one of the horses as well." Mother harrumphed in frustration.

Leo ignored him, less concerned with the comings and goings of a stable lad than Felix's continued absence. A tiny, terrified part of him whispered that perhaps Felix hadn't just gone for a ride, that perhaps he'd packed up and gone for good. But as quickly as the thought surfaced, Leo dismissed it. Felix wouldn't leave without saying goodbye.

At least, he hoped not.

"When did Felix leave, Your Majesty?" Janus asked, and the obvious concern in his voice had the back of Leo's neck prickling.

"It was"—Leo tried to think—"well, it was before the guests arrived."

"Aye," Mother confirmed. "Shadow was already gone when I came down to sort the horses."

Janus's brow furrowed. "He could just be making the most of the sunshine after being cooped up for so long, but it's not like—" He broke off, shading his eyes with one hand, and peered over Leo's shoulder and across the meadow. "All hells," he cursed, and Leo swivelled on his heel to see what had caused his reaction.

His heart dropped into the pit of his stomach at the sight of a horse meandering back towards them, reins dangling loose and no rider in sight.

It was Shadow.

Mother bustled toward the gate and grabbed the horse's reins as soon as Shadow drew close. "It looks like Flick's come off again."

Janus rubbed a hand down the side of his face. "He probably overdid it, the stubborn little shit. I'll go and look for him."

Leo opened his mouth to say that he'd come too, but he was cut off by the sound of hooves thundering against the dirt and a desperate voice calling out, the words lost to wind and distance.

If he squinted, Leo could make out a young man riding toward them like the devil himself was after him, clouds of dust flying up behind him as he leaned forward and spurred his mount on. When he got closer, Leo saw that there was a second figure behind the first—a girl, if the long hair billowing out behind her was any indication.

Beside him, Janus tensed and gripped the handle of his

sword, and Mother grabbed a broad shovel, and, holding it up like a weapon, moved in front of Leo. In that moment, Leo felt both overprotected and underprepared in equal measure.

The horse reached them, hooves clattering against the cobbles and sides heaving as the rider slid from its back, followed by a young girl who Leo vaguely recognised from his trips to the kitchen.

"Davin? What the bloody hell is going on?" Mother barked.

Davin gasped out "Felix!" and the girl let out a soft sob.

"What about Felix?" Leo demanded, his gut churning. He resisted the urge to drag the boy up by his shirtfront, but only barely. "Where is he? Did he fall? Is he hurt?"

"No, sire! He's—someone took him!"

Leo froze.

"What do you *mean*, someone took him? Don't talk nonsense, boy!" Mother said.

"'S true! We saw!" Davin insisted, elbowing his companion, who sniffled and nodded.

Janus put his hands on his knees and crouched so his face was at eye level with the boy. "Davin, is it? Tell me exactly what you saw," he said in a low, even tone, and Leo would have sworn the man was completely calm, if he hadn't seen the tremor in his hands where they were clutching at the fabric of his trousers.

Still, it had the desired effect. Davin drew himself up straight. "Well, I'd taken Maisie out for a ride, and we'd stopped for a bit at that nice stand of trees, and while we were, um, resting, some horses passed us, and when I looked, I saw a man in a black hood and cape, and he had—he had—" His breath caught.

"Deep breath, son." Janus put a hand on his shoulder and gave an encouraging squeeze, and all Leo could think was that the man must have nerves of steel and the patience of a saint.

It did the trick, though, because Davin drew in a breath and continued. "I saw Felix. He was slung over the back of the man's horse, all tied up and hanging there like a sack of spuds, and they went riding off toward Blackmount Ridge!"

"Someone took *Felix?*" Janus sounded equal parts horrified and incredulous, and that, Leo thought, pretty much summed up his own feelings.

"Uh-huh. And…and…" Davin looked down and scuffed his boot in the dirt.

"Out with it, lad," Mother growled.

As an information gathering technique, it worked just as well as Janus's more measured approach. Davin didn't waste any time saying, "Only, I think I recognised the horse from when the visitors were here last. It was…" He bit his lip, ducked his head, and blurted out, "It was Prince Stephan's horse."

*What?*

Leo's mouth dropped open.

"Are you *sure?*" Janus demanded.

Davin nodded vigorously. "I remembered because it has a big mark up one side like lightning, and Ollie and I laughed about how daft it was that the prince had called it Thunder instead of Lightning. It was definitely his horse."

There was a moment's silence while they digested that

information before Janus patted Davin's shoulder again and said quietly, "Thank you, Davin. Can I ask that you and Maisie don't tell anyone else what you saw?"

Maisie gave a solemn nod. Davin mimed twisting a key against his lips, paused, and unlocked them again before saying, "I'm not in trouble for skiving, then?"

"Not this time," Leo said. "Off you go."

Davin's eyes widened at being addressed by the king and he and Maisie scurried away, presumably before Leo changed his mind.

Janus set his shoulders back, his spine ramrod straight and his expression murderous. "That bastard. He has my son, and I'm going after him."

"I'm coming with you."

"Absolutely not," Janus said, and it didn't escape Leo's notice that he didn't bother with niceties. "You'll only slow me down."

Leo glared but Janus remained impassive, and Leo knew that they didn't have time to waste, so in the end he threw his hands in the air. "Fine! But you'll take Mattias and six of your best guards."

Janus cocked an eyebrow. "*All* of my guards are my best guards." He turned on his heel and started jogging towards the castle. Leo followed him.

"Mattias is in the gardens with the princess," he directed, and Janus gave a terse nod and turned up the pathway that led into the ornate arrangement of flower beds. As they reached a solid wooden gate covered with vines, Leo put a hand on Janus's as he went to lift the latch. "Do you think the princess can be trusted?" he said in an undertone.

Janus tilted his head back and looked at the sky, either considering or praying for strength, Leo wasn't sure which. Soon enough, though, Janus gave a decisive nod. "I've spent enough time guarding the princess to know she has no time for her idiot brother and his ideas, so I can't see why she'd have anything to do with this. Whatever scheme Stephan's cooked up, she isn't part of it."

Well, that was something, at least. "But why have they taken Felix?" Leo said, more to himself than anyone as Janus opened the gate.

"Who's taken Felix?" Sophia demanded.

She was seated on a bench, perched next to Mattias under the shade of a tree, but she stood and hurried over.

Mattias followed. "Someone took Flick?" His mouth thinned to a hard line. "Do we know who?"

"One of the boys saw him being carried away unconscious towards Blackmount Ridge. And"—Leo winced internally—"I'm sorry, but he said the horse belonged to Stephan."

He braced himself for Sophia's denial, but she just folded her arms, rolled her eyes in resignation, and said, "Of course my brother's too stupid to use someone else's horse. But the good news is that he lacks imagination as well as stealth, so I know *exactly* where he's taken Felix. There's a hunting lodge that we use there."

She placed a hand on Leo's cheek in reassurance, and there was just enough comfort in the touch to help Leo keep himself together, but not so much that it would shake him apart.

Sophia turned to Mattias. "What do you say, Chancellor? Shall we go and rescue Leo's groom?"

Leo stared, only able to manage a faint, "What?"

Sophia huffed and started walking and talking at the same time, taking long, determined steps as they made their way back to the castle. "It's simple. Stephan obviously figured out there's something between you and Felix, so he's taken him as bait, hoping you'll ride to the rescue. Then he plans to either kidnap or assassinate you. Who knows which?" She shrugged. "It's Stephan. The plan likely doesn't make any sense. The important thing is, you can't be the one to rescue Felix, but Mattias and I can." She paused at the bottom of the staircase long enough to turn and say, "Mattias, you *are* skilled with your blade, aren't you? You seem like you would be."

Inexplicably, Mattias's cheeks turned pink. "I like to think I am," he said gruffly.

"Excellent. Let me go and change out of this"—she waved a hand at her gown—"and I'll lead you to them."

And with that she was off, striding up the staircase as all three men stared after her with something like awe.

## Chapter Fifteen

Felix was woken by a rhythmic thudding that matched the pounding in his head, the creak of leather, and the rich scent of horse. As his consciousness returned, he became aware that there was something binding his wrists and ankles, that his head was hanging low, and that he was tied in place as he bounced along.

Ignoring the hammering in his skull, he opened his eyes only to be met with nothing but darkness. Blindfolded, then.

It all came back to him.

The sudden blow, someone dragging him from his horse and tying him up, and then, when he'd struggled, another whack, harder this time. It must have knocked him out cold because he had no memory of anything after that.

The bouncing continued, the rhythm maddeningly familiar, and when he combined it with the sounds of a saddle, Felix finally figured out that he must be tied across the rear of someone's horse—which meant that he'd been deliberately abducted.

Him—a *nobody*.

There must be a mistake. Some idiot must have seen him riding Shadow and assumed that a horse of that calibre would be carrying someone important. Felix would have laughed out loud, if his head hadn't throbbed quite so much.

He did his best to relax, unwilling to let his captors know he was awake and hopeful that he'd hear something, anything, that would give him a clue as to what was happening. But the rider was mostly silent apart from a few frustrated grunts and clicks of the tongue directed at the horse. Whoever it was, their equestrian skills were basic at best. As time wore on, the dryness in Felix's mouth and the increasing strain on his muscles as he was jostled against the horse's broad back almost tempted him to say something.

But what, exactly, should he say?

*Not to interrupt your plans, but any chance we could stop so I can stretch my legs? Also, could I get a drink and perhaps a sandwich?*

*Was* there such a thing as accepted captivity etiquette?

*Leo would know*, he thought wryly. He'd probably taken lessons in it just in case he was ever kidnapped.

At the thought of Leo, Felix's heart twisted painfully.

If Felix didn't make it back by tonight, how long would Leo wait for him? Would he think Felix had abandoned him? Somehow, picturing Leo waiting in his chambers for a visitor that never came was more distressing than being arse-up over a horse going who knew where, and it didn't take long before Felix found his initial distress and confusion turning to a simmering, self-righteous anger.

How dare someone just...scoop him up like a lost puppy?

He'd had *plans*, and he wasn't going to let some cut-rate body snatcher ruin them. No, he'd been trained by the captain of the guard. Whoever had taken him, Felix was going to make them regret it.

Which, fine, wasn't going to happen right *now*—not while he was trussed up like a prize pig and couldn't see—but once he was untied, *then* he'd make his attackers' lives hell, stage a daring escape, and ride back home to Leo.

Somehow.

True, he didn't exactly have an escape plan, but then again, he was working blind—literally.

He was distracted by the horse underneath him angling up and the sound of hooves scrabbling on rock as they lurched upward. The movement caused him to slip backward, and he squawked in momentary panic.

The ride levelled out and the horse came to a halt. A hand slapped his arse, making him squawk again, in indignation this time.

"So, you're back with us?" a deep voice said. "Just in time. We're here."

Rough hands tugged at the ropes around Felix's waist, and then he was sliding back and down, his legs threatening to fold under him as his feet hit the ground. Someone grasped the front of his shirt and pulled him upright.

"Take him inside," the same voice said.

The ropes around his ankles rasped as they were pulled away and Felix found himself being guided none too gently forward, stumbling over a rocky path. A firm grip on his shoulder held him in place. He heard the creak of a door before he was pulled through a doorway, a stone floor echoing under the soles of his boots.

He was shoved into a seat and his wrists were released and retied to the arms of the chair. He dimly registered that his short sword had been taken, but at least his legs remained free. Felix felt a glimmer of hope. He just needed to distract whoever this was before it occurred to them to tie him up more securely.

"Please," he said. "There's been a mistake. I don't know who you think I am, but I'm just a groom."

"Oh, I know exactly who you are," the voice said as Felix's blindfold was pulled off.

Felix blinked rapidly against the daylight, his eyes taking a moment to adjust. When his vision cleared, he blinked again just to check he was seeing what he thought he was seeing, but the scene in front of him remained the same, as he'd known it would. "Y-your Highness?"

Prince Stephan loomed over Felix, blindfold still in one hand as he took Felix's chin in his other hand and tipped his head back, tilting it from side to side. "Hmmm. I suppose you're pretty enough."

Felix jerked his head back out of the prince's grasp, his heart racing. "I...I don't understand."

But he had an awful, growing suspicion that he did.

Stephan crouched in front of him, so he was at eye level. "Don't you? I'm disappointed. I'd thought you would at least have half a brain in your head. Although, perhaps Leo prefers his bedfellows pretty and dumb."

Felix swallowed. "I don't know what you're talking about."

Stephan gave Felix's cheek a light slap. "Don't play stupid. I saw him fussing over you when you came off your horse. A king doesn't care a fig for the well-being of a groom—but he might care about his *lover*."

Felix tugged at the ropes holding his arms to the chair and felt the tiniest bit of give, which fed his earlier flicker of hope. He didn't know if anybody had noticed he wasn't back from his ride, but eventually someone would come looking. And meanwhile, if he could just keep Stephan talking, he was confident he could work himself free, or at the very least buy himself some time. He might not know anything about kidnap etiquette, but his father had made sure he was well educated in the art of self-defence—and that included escape.

"I don't understand," he said again, flexing his forearms.

Stephan straightened and folded his arms over his chest, and out of the corner of his eye Felix spotted two other men circling around behind him.

Stephan smirked. "You, boy, are the reason Leopold turned down my sister. Their marriage would have been a milestone and joined our kingdoms. But your king wasn't interested, and at first, I didn't understand why he'd walk away from such an advantageous alliance. But when I saw how he fussed over you after my men aimed badly enough to unseat you instead of the king"—he shot a glare over Felix's shoulder—"I realised that the reason for his refusal was simple. He's in love with *you*."

"No, he's not," Felix said, and he forced a note of bitterness into his voice. "I'm just a convenient fuck."

He didn't really think it was true, not with how devastated Leo had looked when he'd left, but he also didn't want to give Stephan any reason to think he was anything other than a warm body.

"And yet he had you staying in the castle after your fall," Stephan said, tapping a fingertip against his chin and pacing up and down in front of Felix's chair.

"Why were you shooting at the king in the first place?" Felix asked, hoping to divert Stephan from following that thought to its logical conclusion.

"It was meant to be a near miss, perhaps a flesh wound. A reminder that Lilleforth is in the precarious position of having no heir should something happen to the king. Then someone would whisper in Leo's ear that perhaps he should marry Sophia after all, just in case."

"And who was going to say that, exactly?" Felix said, ignoring the fact that he'd said almost the same thing, although from a very different viewpoint.

Stephan arched an eyebrow in a way that was probably meant to be imposing, but fell short. "It's easy to find someone who's willing to perform certain services: tell a king what you need him to hear, pass on information, that sort of thing. How do you think I knew you'd recovered at the castle?"

Felix's gut soured at the idea that someone had been watching Leo—watching *him*—without him knowing. But he kept the shock off his face and reminded himself that spies were common, and that Stephan was, first and foremost, an idiot. Felix just needed to keep him talking while he worked on his ropes—and Felix was an *expert* at talking.

He gave a lazy half shrug. "I assumed you'd have spies. Doesn't everybody? It's just a shame yours are so terrible at their job."

Stephan's brow creased. "If they're so terrible, how did I know you'd gone riding today?"

Felix shrugged again, as much as his bonds would let him, and took the opportunity to tug at his ropes, loosening them further. "Maybe you *didn't* know. Maybe, because I've been in bed for over a week, you took a lucky guess that I'd want to ride. Or maybe you've been holed up in this"—he looked around, took in the large single room with stag heads on the wall and a stone fireplace, and made an educated guess—"hunting lodge, having someone keep watch on the stables, waiting for any sign of me, because you couldn't figure out a way to take me from the castle. Which, I'm still not clear on why you took me at all? Why *am* I here?"

"Because Leo *loves* you," Stephan repeated, and Felix wasn't sure if hearing it hurt because it was a lie, or because it might be the truth. "I considered just killing you and removing the object of his affections permanently, but there was no guarantee he wouldn't declare war as an act of revenge. So instead, I thought I'd take you just to show that I can, and then I'd have my men hurt you before sending you back with a message. If Leo wants to keep you safe, he'll marry my sister. And if she's Queen of Lilleforth, she can't inherit the throne of Evergreen—which means it will come to me."

Felix blinked. "That is...the stupidest plan I've ever heard."

It was actually far more clever than Felix had expected from Stephan, but he wasn't admitting that.

Stephan pursed his lips. "I don't know. Holding Leo and his future actions hostage over his misplaced affection for a stable boy? It seems quite effective to me."

"I'm not a stable boy! I'm the *royal groom*, thank you very much, and I think you might have forgotten something when you hatched your brainless scheme," Felix said, hands curling into fists against the wooden arms of the chair as he tensed his forearms again and was rewarded for his efforts with a significant slackening of his bonds.

"What is it that you think I've forgotten?" Stephan demanded, eyes narrowing.

"Oh, just that your plan is pointless because it was *Sophia* who turned Leo down. Leo didn't get any say in it."

"Impossible," Stephan declared, but he sounded uncertain.

"Maybe she didn't bother telling you, which wouldn't surprise me, honestly. You're the younger sibling—unimportant, whatever you tell yourself. Unless, of course, you were stupid enough to hurt the king's lover. If Leo *does* have feelings for me as you claim, he'll hunt you down himself. You're painting a target on your back, and it's all for nothing, because Sophia won't marry Leo no matter what you do."

Gods, Felix hoped that sounded more convincing to Stephan than it did to him.

One of his guards cleared his throat. "He might have a point."

Stephan glared at him. "Well, nobody asked you, did they?"

Felix huffed out a tired sigh. He was at the end of his patience. "Listen, hell hath no fury like a woman scorned—unless it's an entitled king who's been deprived of his favourite plaything. Which, right now, is me. Remind me again. How many men do you have? Two?"

Stephan bit his lip. "You make a good point."

*Well, thank fuck for that.*

"So, you'll let me go?"

"What? Oh, no. It's just that if I let you live, you'll tell Leo I was behind your disappearance, so it's best to just kill you. It's easy enough to make it look like a riding accident."

"Oh, you don't want to do that," Felix said hastily. "But if you let me go, I could pretend I took a fall and had to walk back, how embarrassing, ha-ha, and never mention this at all."

Stephan turned his cold gaze on Felix and his eyes narrowed. "No, you're right. Sending you back injured could work against me. Better just to dispose of you altogether. And who knows, perhaps my sister can provide some comfort to the king in his grief, and they can be persuaded to marry after all."

Felix couldn't help the eye roll. "Gods, your sister got the brains *and* the looks in your family, didn't she? She doesn't *want* to marry Leo. She will *never* want to marry Leo."

There was a moment of silence when Felix thought perhaps his argument had worked, but then Stephan said, "A blow to the head, I think. That will look like your mount kicked you."

Felix's heart raced as he realised Stephan was serious.

It was time to put his father's training into action. He checked that his ropes were sufficiently loose, braced himself, and then hurled his entire body backward, chair and all, wincing when his shoulders slammed against the stone floor. He was rewarded with the sound of timber splintering. The ropes holding him in place burned against his skin as he yanked on them, but with one final pull they snapped and he was finally, blessedly free.

He rolled out of the wreckage of the chair and scrambled to his feet before the guards had even realised what was happening, and he didn't hesitate to grab the biggest piece of timber he could find. He hefted the chair leg in his hand before swinging with speed and precision, hitting Stephan solidly across the side of his head. Stephan's eyes widened and he clutched at the injury, staggering. Blood seeped between his fingers and Felix swung again, harder this time, catching Stephan's hand where it was pressed to his face and making him howl.

*Third time's the charm,* Felix thought grimly and wasted no time in delivering one more blow, putting all his force behind it. Stephan yelped and crumpled to the ground, his hand twitching against the stone floor like a dying spider.

Felix spun on his heel, still clutching his weapon and ready to take on the two guards, but as it turned out, he didn't need to. At that moment the door crashed open to reveal Mattias, Sophia, and his father with a contingent of guards.

"Dad!" Felix said brightly. "It looks like all that time in the training yards paid off after all! You could take care of those two for me, though." He nodded at Stephan's men, his chest heaving with exertion and exhilaration, and while he knew he was grinning like a madman, he couldn't seem to help it.

At a signal from Mattias, the guards made quick work of restraining Stephan's henchmen, who didn't seem inclined to resist. His dad crossed the room in three long strides, pulling Felix close and hugging him tight as the chair leg clattered to the ground. "Gods, Flick, are you all right? What happened?"

"Oh, you know. Stephan wanted the throne of Evergreen, so he thought he could get Leo to marry Sophia by threatening me, and because he's an idiot he forgot that I'm the king's guard, not just his—"

"*Felix.*"

"—*groom.* What did you think I was going to say, Dad?"

His dad squeezed him tighter before letting him go with a sigh that was two parts affection, one part exasperation. "Honestly, son, who knows with you?" He pulled back and looked Felix up and down. "Did they hurt you?" he asked, brow creased.

Felix rolled his shoulders, taking stock. He ached from hitting the stone floor, and his muscles were stiff from being slung over the arse of a horse while trussed up, but other than that, he didn't think he had any injuries. "Not really. Just a bump to the head."

Sophia stepped forward and prodded Stephan with a toe. "Have you killed my brother, do you think?" she asked in the tone of someone discussing the weather.

Felix took a moment to look at her properly. She was dressed in a fitted shirt and trousers that were a far cry from her normal gowns, and riding boots rather than dainty embroidered slippers. With her red hair twisted into a tight coil and a sword in her hand, she looked for all the world like an avenging angel.

"I don't...think so?" Felix said, as it occurred to him that perhaps he shouldn't have hit Stephan *quite* so hard, what with him being a prince and all.

Sophia let out a sigh. "That's probably for the best." She prodded Stephan harder with her boot, and when she received an answering groan, she asked, "Stephan, why have you kidnapped the king's lover?" Her tone dripped condescension and menace.

Stephan moaned again.

Sophia rolled her eyes. "You always were a dramatic child. You barely have a scratch." Stephan raised his head and Sophia responded by pointing her sword at his midsection. "Stay there while I decide what to do with you."

Stephan whimpered but didn't move.

Sophia turned her head. "Mattias, can you take Felix home? The captain and I can deal with this...mess." She gestured vaguely with the hand not holding a sword to her brother's soft parts.

"Of course, ma'am," Mattias said. The soft smile on his face seemed out of place given the situation—but then, Felix was still grinning like a loon right now, so who was he to judge?

A part of Felix would have liked to stay and see what happened, but from the vengeful glint in Sophia's eye—

and his father's, too—he got the feeling it was best if he was as far removed from the scene as possible.

And besides, now that the first rush of victorious hand-to-hand combat—or hand-to-chair-leg combat, if you wanted to be picky—was wearing off, Felix was *tired*.

He wanted to go home.

He nodded his readiness to Mattias, and they made their way out the door. Felix paused as something struck him. "I don't know what happened to Shadow," he said, his voice cracking. He wasn't sure why the fate of his horse was hitting him so hard under the circumstances, since someone had threatened to *kill* him today for heaven's sake, but at the same time he was overwhelmed with a sense of loss, and he found himself on the verge of tears.

It was *embarrassing*.

"He's fine, Flick," Mattias said. He spoke quietly, like Felix was a horse that he was trying not to spook. "He came back on his own."

Relief flooded through Felix at hearing that, and he let out a shaky exhale.

"Get on behind me." Mattias mounted his horse, and Felix hauled himself up behind him, leaning his head against Mattias's shoulder. "Let's get you home. There's a certain someone who'll be desperate to see you."

"If he's so desperate, why isn't he here?" Felix muttered. "Or does he only care enough to send the hired help?"

Mattias tensed, his shoulders stiffening.

Felix immediately wanted to take the words back. He cursed his runaway mouth. "No, Mattias, I didn't mean—I'm so grateful you came for me. I just, I…" He trailed off.

"You thought he'd be the one to rescue you," Mattias said, and his tone told Felix that he understood.

"Yes," Felix mumbled, knowing how stupid that was. "But it's not like he would have. We're just—"

"Felix, the *only* reason Leo isn't here himself is because I threatened to tie him to the bed, and not in the way you like."

Felix lifted his head the tiniest bit. "Really?"

Mattias let out a fond chuckle. "He was beside himself when he discovered you were gone. Your father and Sophia refused to let him come along and he wasn't brave enough to cross the pair of them, but he was desperate to be your knight in shining armour. He was pouting like a child when we left, and I had to put a guard on him to make sure he didn't follow."

Felix could picture it. The very thought of Leo being willing to come for him filled him with warmth, and he was overcome with a deep, aching need to see his king.

"Can we go?" he said. "I need to tell Leo something."

Mattias hummed and flicked the reins. His horse moved forward at a steady pace and as they made their way back, Felix found that he felt better with every step that took him closer to home, closer to Leo.

Closer to confessing the truth.

Because now he understood *why* Leo had been trying to tell him how he felt earlier. Felix hadn't wanted to hear it then, but that was before that brief window of time today when Felix had seriously considered that he might be leaving the hunting lodge as a corpse.

Because he'd realised, in those few stark moments, that

if he *did* die, his one regret would be never getting to tell Leo how he felt.

This wasn't just a fling anymore, not for him. Felix wasn't stupid, and he knew that he and Leo could never amount to anything, but he needed to *say* it, just once.

He needed to tell Leo that he loved him.

## Chapter Sixteen

Leo paced the length of the rug in his office. Then he paced it again.

It had been hours since the rescue party had left, and now the first soft streaks of pink were creeping across the summer sky and ushering in the end of the day, and they *still* weren't back.

Whoever had first said no news was good news had been a damned liar, because the longer Leo didn't hear anything, the more he was convinced that the worst had happened, and the waiting and worrying had him almost vibrating out of his skin. He was frankly terrified of what Stephan had planned for Felix, and with every minute that passed, he felt hope slipping away as the prospect of Felix coming to real harm loomed larger.

He circled around to the window that overlooked the courtyard and stared into the distance looking for any signs of movement before running a hand through his hair and flinging the door open.

The guard posted to his door, a giant bear of a man, stepped in front of the open doorway.

"Can I assist Your Majesty?"

"I wish to go to the stables," Leo said, jutting his chin out. "I'm going to look for them."

The guard, Thomas, stayed blocking Leo's exit, arms folded over his big, barrelled chest. "I'm afraid the chancellor's instructions were clear, Your Majesty," he said calmly. "You're to remain within the castle."

"Do as I say! I am the *king*," Leo snapped.

"Of course, Your Majesty, which is why you must be protected at all costs," Thomas said, unmoving.

Leo's shoulders sagged and he ran a hand through his hair again. He changed tactics, putting on his most crestfallen expression. "Are you *sure* I can't ride out just a few miles?" he wheedled. "It's been an *age* since they left, so they're probably almost back. I wouldn't be putting myself in danger just going to meet them."

"I'm sorry, sire," Thomas said, "but I was given specific instructions by the chancellor, the captain of the guard, *and* the Princess of Evergreen, and they all said you weren't to ride anywhere. It's more than my job's worth." He set his hands behind his back and spread his legs wide in a resting position that indicated he planned to stay right there in Leo's doorway like a giant inconvenient roadblock, and Leo knew he wouldn't be getting past the man any time soon.

Leo harrumphed and swung the door shut, and he could have sworn he saw a hint of amusement on the man's face before the door slammed on him.

Damn Mattias and his overprotectiveness, and damn

Janus Hobson as well for agreeing with him. This was the third time in as many hours that Leo had attempted to ride out, and Thomas had been just as implacable in his refusal this last time as he had been the first two—which was probably why Mattias had chosen him.

Leo wasn't sure which rankled more—that Mattias had assumed Leo would need supervision, or the fact that he was *right*.

Because while Leo *knew* it was only sensible for him to stay behind rather than risk his safety, that didn't lessen the temptation to saddle up Blackbird and set out on his own. It was doubtless why Thomas had been charged with preventing him from doing that very thing.

But he couldn't be expected to just wait around, surely? Not when Felix had been *kidnapped?*

He groaned and ran a hand down his face, then opened the door again. "Apologies, Thomas."

Thomas dipped his head. "No apology needed, sire."

"No." Leo sighed. "I'm impatient, that's all."

"I hadn't noticed," Thomas said, straight-faced, and Leo made a mental note to arrange for him to get some sort of bonus, while wondering who it was that was responsible for hiring staff with attitude.

Mattias, probably.

He left the door open just so he didn't feel so entombed, and went back to staring out the window and worrying.

The fact he and Felix had parted on bad terms didn't help. Leo deeply regretted now that he hadn't told Felix how he felt, even if Felix hadn't been able to say it back. The thought that he might not get another chance, and that Felix might die without knowing that Leo loved him, was unbearable.

Because Leo *did* love his groom. It was indisputable. And yes, it was messy and unconventional and inconvenient, and Leo wasn't sure what it meant in practical terms, but he found he didn't really care.

He only knew that Felix was everything he'd ever wanted, and he'd do anything to keep him.

He continued to stare out the window. It didn't register at first that there was something moving on the horizon, but then the movement caught his attention. "Thomas!"

"Yes, sire?" Thomas hurried over.

"Is...who's that?" he demanded as he pointed at a small, slow-moving speck, hope bubbling up in his chest. "Is that the chancellor?" Not that he really needed the confirmation. After all these years, he'd know the set of Mattias's long body on horseback anywhere, even at a distance.

Thomas shaded his eyes and hummed. "It...yes, I think it is, sire. And there's someone else as well."

Leo looked again as they drew closer, and yes, there was a lean, dark-haired figure plastered against Mattias's back, and his heart raced at the sight. "It's them! It's Mattias and Felix!"

He turned and went haring out the door and down the stairs, ignoring Thomas's calls of, "Sire! Sire, *wait!*"

He'd waited long enough.

Leo had made it as far as the gates of the courtyard by the time Thomas caught up, and Mattias was close enough that even in the dim light of dusk, Leo could make him out clearly. Mattias spurred his horse on to a trot and within minutes he was right in front of Leo and dismounting with ease, and there, sliding out of the saddle right after him, was—

"Felix! You're safe!"

The words left Leo in a rush. Relief washed over him like an ocean wave and all the tension left his body. Felix gave him a crooked grin and stepped forward, and Leo cupped his face in both hands, tilting his jaw from side to side and checking him for any sign of injury.

As if reading his thoughts, Felix said, "I'm fine. Just a bump on the head where Stephan's men clocked me one."

"Shall I send for the maester?" Leo asked, hands fluttering over Felix's shirt as he tried to touch him everywhere and check he was really all right.

Felix clamped a warm hand over his, stilling it and giving him a look that reflected the same yearning that Leo felt. "I don't need the maester, Leo. I need *you*." And with that, he leaned in and kissed Leo in a desperate, messy clash of teeth and tongues. Leo kissed him right back, not caring that they were where anyone could see, not caring about anything at all except that Felix was here, whole and safe and *his*.

"I love you," Leo whispered against Felix's lips, unable to hold the words in any longer.

Felix pulled back, eyes wide. "What?"

"I love you," Leo repeated, throwing caution to the winds, because suddenly the most important thing in the world was telling Felix how he felt. "You are my treasure and my delight, and you own my heart."

Felix's face lit up. "And I love you. Thank the gods you feel the same, because for a minute there I really did think I was going to die, and my biggest regret was that I hadn't gotten to tell you how I feel, but I love you, I do, and I know it can never work, but—"

Leo shut him up with another kiss, soft and tender, and when they parted, he pushed a stray curl behind Felix's ear. "I love you, Flick. We'll *make* it work."

Leo didn't know *how* they'd make it work, but that didn't matter right now. The important thing was that Felix had said he *loved* him, and it was more than Leo had dared hope for.

They could worry about the details later.

Leo trailed his fingertips downward until he was cupping Felix's cheek, and Felix leaned into his touch with a tiny sigh. That small sound was enough to make Leo's earlier protectiveness surge back to life. He needed to get his boy alone, to run his hands over every inch of Felix's bare skin and reassure himself that Felix really was unharmed— and then kiss him all over as well, just to be certain. He leaned in and rested his head against the curve of Felix's throat, only to pull back as the stench of horse and anxious sweat assailed his senses. "Gods, but you stink!"

Felix's mouth quirked. "Oh, I'm sorry. Next time I'm kidnapped I'll be sure to stop for a wash once I've knocked out my assailant."

"Brat," Leo muttered, but he relaxed at hearing Felix make light of his ordeal. He reached out and ran a thumb down his cheekbone, unable to keep his hands to himself. "Did you really knock him out?"

"Of course." Felix shrugged. "You forget, I train three times a week with the guards, and my dad doesn't go easy."

And the thing was, in his worry, Leo *had* sort of forgotten that Felix was a skilled fighter, because he associated him with sex and laughter and spankings, but of *course* his boy could look after himself. That was why he was Leo's bodyguard, after all.

The idea of Felix taking on his attackers and winning was incredibly arousing, and Leo stepped closer, ignoring the smell, and murmured, "My brave warrior. You are *so* attractive to me right now."

Felix laughed softly.

Leo turned to Mattias, ignoring the small crowd of onlookers from the castle who had gathered in the courtyard. "I need a bath sent up to my room. Can you arrange it, Matty?"

"Of course," Mattias said, his smile soft. "Will you need dinner sent up as well?"

Leo shook his head. "We'll stop by the kitchens."

Mattias nodded and slipped away into the castle, presumably to arrange the bath, and Leo followed him inside with one arm wrapped around Felix's waist, keeping him close as he guided him toward the kitchens.

The cook fussed suitably over Felix and fed them both, and by the time they'd eaten and made it to Leo's rooms, there was an enormous copper tub filled with steaming water set in front of the fireplace, where the flames crackled merrily.

Felix gave a pleased hum at the sight of it. "Oh, that does look good." He peeled out of his shirt and Leo was glad to see that Felix hadn't been lying. There weren't any new injuries of note, just the red marks around his wrists where he'd been tied up, and the last fading traces of his earlier bruises.

He reached out and ran his fingertips lightly up Felix's ribs and down again, and Felix stood still, letting him touch. "I really am fine, Leo," he said softly.

"Hush and let me look at you," Leo admonished, tugging at the laces of Felix's trousers and pushing them down his legs until they puddled around his ankles.

Felix shoved his smallclothes down as well and stepped out of the whole mess, and Leo was struck anew with how beautiful he was. He reached out a hand and Felix took it.

Leo led him over to the bathtub and Felix lowered himself into the water, letting out a low moan as he submerged himself. "Fuck, that's good. Everything aches."

Leo tensed. "You said you weren't hurt!"

Felix opened his eyes just long enough to roll them. "I said I wasn't *injured*. But my muscles are still stiff. I just got bounced halfway to kingdom come hogtied and slung across the back of a horse, then I threw myself onto a stone floor hard enough to break the chair I was tied to, and then I sat on the back of *another* horse to get back to you, and it wasn't exactly comfortable sharing a saddle with Mattias and his stupidly long legs." He shrugged, causing the water to slosh, and closed his eyes again.

When Felix put it like that, Leo was forced to admit that perhaps he was overreacting the tiniest bit. He wanted to know the details of how, exactly, Felix had escaped, but he could tell that now wasn't the time to ask, so instead he lowered himself to his knees next to the tub. After soaping up the washcloth, he dragged it across Felix's shoulders, leaving a trail of suds in its wake. Felix hummed and leaned forward to give him better access, and Leo continued to wash his bare skin.

He'd never bathed anyone before—it wasn't something kings did—but he must have been doing a reasonable job if the soft hums and noises of appreciation Felix was making were any indication. He worked his way down Felix's back and across his chest, before pausing to tilt Felix's head back and wet his hair with warm water from the jug the maids had left for that purpose. Felix blinked the water away and when he opened his eyes, the droplets caught on his lashes glistened like tiny diamonds. It was so utterly charming that Leo gave into temptation and leaned in to press their lips together.

Felix smiled against his mouth and tangled one wet hand in Leo's hair, holding him there as he deepened the kiss, tongue darting out and teasing against the seam of Leo's mouth. Leo let him in, and they stayed that way, tongues tangling as they kissed soft and lazy, until Felix drew back with a satisfied hum.

Leo found himself unable to stop touching Felix. He ran his fingertips through the damp curls at the nape of Felix's neck until Felix sighed and said, "Stop. If you keep doing that, I'll fall asleep, and I don't *want* to fall asleep. I have plans involving the man I love."

"Say that again," Leo said, a thrill running through him at the words.

Felix rolled his eyes, but he was smiling. "The man I love. Which is you. Happy?"

"Very," Leo said. "Now tell me about these plans."

Felix hummed. "Well, you've just washed me all over in a most arousing fashion, and it's been *far* too long since your hands were on my skin. I think you can guess." He grabbed Leo's wrist and guided it under the surface of the water to his cock, which was hard against Leo's palm.

Heat raced through Leo and his own cock throbbed with want. He stroked Felix's erection just enough to elicit a whimper before standing and holding out a hand. Felix flashed him a mischievous smile and allowed himself to be helped out of the tub. Leo's breath caught in his throat when he saw Felix's cock standing proud and flushed against the pale skin of his belly. Felix's eyes were bright, and his wet skin gleamed in the firelight. "What do you think?" he teased as he picked up a towel, rubbing it over his body in the barest approximation of drying himself before letting it drop to the floor. "Am I fit to grace the bed of a king?"

"Only *this* king," Leo growled out.

Felix laughed softly and Leo suspected he was mocking him, but he found he didn't care, too intent on getting Felix into his bed and putting his hands all over him. He stepped forward and cupped the globes of Felix's arse. Felix gave a soft moan and his eyelids fluttered closed as Leo relished the press of warm skin against his palms, and then Felix was kissing him, his hands plucking at Leo's damp shirt. "Off," he murmured against Leo's mouth.

Leo pulled away so he could undress, and as soon as he was naked, Felix was gliding his hands over Leo's belly, up and across his shoulders, and down to his hips. Leo shivered under his touch, soaking up the contact. He buried his face in the curve of Felix's throat and pressed soft kisses against the damp skin, and Felix let out a low groan.

Leo turned them and directed them to the bed and

Felix went willingly, falling back against the mattress with Leo on top of him. Leo ground against him, the already-damp head of his cock slip-sliding in the crease of Felix's hip.

Leo reached between them and lined their cocks up properly at the same time as Felix rolled his hips chasing more contact. His length was hot and slippery and utterly divine as it slid against Leo's. Their bodies settled into a messy rhythm, every drag of skin on skin perfect, and heat pooled low in Leo's belly. He wrapped his hand around both their lengths and stroked, and the touch sent lightning racing up his spine. Felix bucked up into his hand, wrapping his arms around Leo's back and pulling him closer. Leo worked their cocks expertly, and it wasn't long before Felix let out a choked-off whine and tensed, pulsing in Leo's hand as he spilled, his entire body drawn taut.

At the sight of Felix with his spine arched, head thrown back, and lips parted, the tension in Leo's belly coiled tighter and tighter until he couldn't have held back his release if his life had depended on it. His balls throbbed and he buried his face against Felix's throat, gave one final, firm stroke, and came with a groan. He gasped and shuddered his way through it, shocked by the intensity of his orgasm, until finally he collapsed, loose-limbed and spent.

They rolled onto their sides and lay together like that, tangled and sated and half-asleep, listening to the crackle of the fireplace, and Leo thought he might quite like to stay like this forever.

## Chapter Seventeen

Felix woke to soft kisses on the nape of his neck and Leo's arm around his waist. As he surfaced to consciousness properly, he smiled into the darkness when he remembered the events of the day before.

Not the attempted kidnapping—he could have done without *that* particular adventure, thank you very much—but afterwards, when Leo had called Felix his delight and his treasure and declared that he loved him. That alone had been worth putting up with the other nonsense for.

He sighed contentedly as Leo tugged him closer, filling any tiny bit of space between their bodies.

"Good morning, my love," Leo rasped, voice rough with sleep, and a thrill ran down Felix's spine.

*My love.*

Would Felix ever get tired of hearing that? He doubted it.

Leo peppered the back of his neck with more tiny kisses, sliding the hand that had been resting on Felix's belly up and over the planes of his chest where it lingered to give a playful tug on Felix's nipple. The sweet sting had Felix arching into the touch, which meant his arse was pressed against Leo's rapidly hardening cock.

Leo tugged at his nipple again and Felix let out a soft groan, rolling his hips instinctively as his own cock thickened. Then Leo was gone, rolling away, but before Felix's sleep-addled brain had time to make sense of it, he was back. He slid an oil-slick finger between Felix's arse cheeks. "Yes?" he murmured, hand stilling.

Felix's breath hitched and he let out a soft, "Please?"

Leo eased the tip of his finger inside and slid it in and out in a series of slow, careful movements, a gentle stretch, before adding a second finger and working him properly open with a steady motion, rubbing against the sensitive nerve endings of Felix's entrance in a delicious tease. Felix rocked back, desperate, and Leo didn't make him wait, setting the broad head of his cock against Felix's entrance and easing into him with a low moan.

Leo pressed forward, one long, even stroke, and Felix relished the heat and length of him. Leo rolled his hips and fucked him slow and gentle like they had all the time in the world, and it felt...intimate, in a way it hadn't been before.

Maybe, Felix reflected, the difference was knowing Leo loved him.

Whatever the reason, Felix closed his eyes and let himself get lost in the rhythmic, sensual rocking of their bodies, and after three long weeks of near abstinence, he relished the tender ache in his arse that told him Leo was where he needed to be. His own arousal grew with every brush of Leo's cock over that sweet spot inside, and he wrapped a hand around his length, which throbbed under his touch. It only took a few strokes before his gut tightened, his nerves tingling as he felt himself getting close. His arse clenched reflexively, and he gasped out, "More."

"With pleasure, sweetheart," Leo purred and mouthed at the curve of his neck, nipping at the skin. The gentle, rolling motion of his hips turned into short, urgent thrusts that stretched and filled Felix perfectly and had him panting, his body drawn as tight as a bowstring. When Leo drove into him *hard*, grasping his hips, tensing, and shuddering, it was enough that Felix came undone, spilling over his hand. His heart thundered in his chest, mind and body flooding with pleasure until he was light-headed with it.

Felix floated, aware of nothing but his cock pulsing out the last of his orgasm and the heat of Leo's body against his back. Long minutes passed—or perhaps it was hours, Felix couldn't quite tell—but as sleep threatened to claim him again, he remembered that he was meant to leave before dawn. Except, he wasn't sure he could bring himself to get out of bed. "I don't want to go," he mumbled.

Leo gave a quiet chuckle. "Well, I'm not planning on *letting* you go any time soon, my love."

Felix's insides warmed at the endearment. "You keep calling me that."

"I do, because you are."

"You called me your delight, yesterday. I liked it."

"That's because everything about you delights me. Shall I make it an official title, and appoint you the King's Delight?"

Felix huffed out a laugh of his own. "I don't need a bollocksy title, thank you. Besides, what happened to discretion?"

"I think discretion became a thing of the past when you kissed me in the courtyard, darling."

Felix tensed as he remembered that he *had* kissed Leo in front of everyone, and it hadn't even occurred to him to ask first. He was suddenly more alert as the enormity of what he'd done hit him. "Gods, you're right, and everybody saw. I'm so sorry."

Leo shifted behind him, his softening cock slipping from Felix's body. He turned Felix in his arms so they were facing and pressed a kiss to the top of his hair. "Felix, I don't care who knows about us. I'm done with discretion, and I'm done with not being able to have the man I love beside me. And the man I love is *you*."

"And I love you, and I don't care who knows it," Felix said. Now that he was assured that he hadn't committed some unforgivable faux pas, happiness bubbled up in his chest at Leo's easy admission.

"Then it's settled." Leo rolled onto his back and pulled Felix so his head was resting on his chest, and Felix stayed there, listening to Leo's heartbeat in the darkness, and wished it were that simple.

Because Felix knew that Leo meant every word he said, but he also wasn't a fool, and he could feel the shadow of Leo's obligations lengthening, getting bigger with every passing moment. He lay there in the quiet until he couldn't stand it any longer before he blurted out, "But if you *did* need to marry and produce an heir, as long as your queen was aware of our arrangement, I—" He took a deep breath and forced the words out. "I'd be prepared to share you."

Leo stiffened beneath him. "What are you talking about?"

Felix closed his eyes and wished he was a better liar. "Marriage. An heir. If that's what needs to happen and if your bride knows it's just an arrangement, you have my blessing."

Leo gave a huff and propped himself on his elbows, dislodging Felix from his spot. "You don't mean that. I saw how jealous you were of Sophia."

"I'm not saying I'd *like* it, but I thought a lot about the ways we could be together on the ride back with Mattias, and I can't see any way past you marrying. So, I've decided that sharing your affection is better than not getting to have you at all."

He was *such* a liar.

In fact, Felix would rather that Leo's bollocks shrivelled up and dropped off than let anyone else get near them—and he *really* liked Leo's bollocks—but he resisted the urge to say so. And in any event, it proved unnecessary because Leo sighed and ran a hand through Felix's hair. "I'm not marrying, sweetheart."

Felix's insides unclenched a little at the statement. In all honesty he wasn't sure he *could* take it if Leo decided to wed. Still, Leo made it sound as if his decision was cut and dried, and if there was one thing that Felix knew, it was that things were *rarely* cut and dried, especially where royalty was concerned. He sat up. "But—"

Leo sat and reached over, cupping Felix's face in his hands and kissing him passionately, cutting off whatever he'd been about to say. When he pulled back, he pressed their foreheads together. "Felix, I love you. When I thought I'd lost you, I vowed that if you came back to me, I wouldn't risk losing you again. And you don't seem like the type who would be happy sharing."

"I'm not," Felix admitted.

"Then marriage is off the table, heir be damned. I'll let the throne go to Evan if it comes to it. I won't care. I'll be dead."

Felix grinned, his heart skipping a beat as affection and relief overwhelmed him. "That is either the most romantic or the most macabre declaration of love I've ever heard."

Leo laughed softly. "Let's call it romantic. Now let me clean you up." He let go of Felix's face and climbed out of bed, and when he returned, he had a damp cloth. Felix let Leo wipe away his release, shivering at the coolness against his skin. "You know, this really is a delectable arse. I can't wait to give it a thorough spanking," Leo mused as he discarded the cloth and rubbed his palms up Felix's thighs and over his cheeks, giving a light slap that made Felix shiver for a completely different reason.

He couldn't wait to be back over Leo's knee and under his hand. "Perhaps I'll be extremely rude today and you'll have to remind me of my place," he said, grinning into the pillow.

"Oh, I foresee a good, hard reminder in your future," Leo said lowly. "But for now, it's not yet dawn. Shall we go back to sleep?" He turned Felix onto his side, plastered himself along his back, and threw an arm over him.

"Mmm," Felix hummed. His eyes were already closing, the early hour and his post-orgasmic haze conspiring to draw him under. He smiled and let himself drift, knowing that Leo would still be there when he woke.

The next time Felix woke up, it was to someone knocking on the door. He patted blindly at the bed, but there was only a warm patch where Leo should have been.

When he opened his eyes, he saw that it was full daylight and Leo was shrugging into his dressing gown and hastening toward the door. He pulled it open a scant inch and told whoever it was, "Go away."

A deep voice Felix recognised as Mattias said, "You can't just stay in your room, Leo. We have things to discuss."

"Felix is still asleep."

"I'm not surprised, after his ordeal."

"Falling in love with me is not an *ordeal*, thank you very much!" Leo huffed.

"I meant the kidnapping," Mattias said, amusement clear in his tone. "And we *do* need to talk about this."

"There's nothing to discuss. I'm keeping him."

Felix sat up in bed and called out, "I'm not a stray kitten from the barns, Leo."

Mattias chuckled. "Sounds like your boy's awake."

Felix shuffled out of bed and retrieved his trousers, dragging them on and collecting his shirt, because one audience with Mattias while naked in Leo's bed was *plenty*, thank you very much.

"Let him in, Leo. He's right. We have things to talk about." He stretched his arms over his head and arched his spine, letting out a yawn before going to join Leo at the door. He wrapped an arm around Leo's shoulders and gave him a peck on the cheek, just because he could, and Leo's expression softened.

Mattias stepped inside and gave Felix a tiny nod. "Your father and the princess returned last night, both of them unharmed."

"Thank you." Felix hadn't really held any concerns for his father's safety, but it was nice to have it confirmed. "And the idiot prince?"

Mattias's smile held a hint of dark satisfaction. "He's currently in the dungeons. A message has been sent to King Andros informing him of Stephan's attempted regicide, and he'll be sent home in disgrace. Sophia tells me he's always been a power-hungry thorn in her father's side, so the king will probably use this as an excuse to banish him. She's going to suggest he be posted to supervise the pig farming district in the furthest corner of the kingdom, as a permanent role. Apparently, he hates pigs."

"Sophia?" Leo said, eyebrows rising. "On a first-name basis now, are we?"

Mattias flushed. "She said I wasn't to bother with her title, and one doesn't cross a woman like that."

Felix took a moment to pull his shirt over his head before saying, "She is rather impressive."

"She's *magnificent*." Mattias breathed out. He stared at nothing for a moment before coming back to himself and clearing his throat. "Anyway. Sophia assures me that there will be no repercussions for Felix beating the prince half to death with a chair leg, given the circumstances."

"He had it coming," Felix said, completely unrepentant.

Leo rolled his eyes. "Well, thank you for letting us

know, but whatever else we need to talk about can wait. I'm going back to bed now and so is Felix. It's the crack of dawn."

"It's almost noon," Mattias said, a smile playing round the corners of his mouth.

"Is it? Are you sure?" Leo looked genuinely surprised, and Felix found himself charmed by this cranky, flustered, just-awake version of his lover.

"Shall we get you something to eat and let you wake up properly?" Felix said soothingly, and Leo gave him a grateful smile.

"I'll have your valet bring a tray up, but then I really do need to see you in my office. Shall we say an hour?" Mattias asked.

"I suppose." Leo sighed. "But what's so important it can't wait?"

"Oh, nothing. Just a solution to the issue of your succession," Mattias said.

"You'd better not have a bride in there, because I'm not doing that," Leo said, the stern effect of his hands on his hips slightly spoiled by his sleep-mussed hair and bare feet.

"Not a bride, no. You'll see. One hour," Mattias said, eyes sparkling, and with that he turned and strode out of the room.

∼

An hour later, Mattias opened the door to his offices and ushered them both inside. Felix had been hesitant about going with Leo, but Leo had said, "I'm not letting you out of my sight, sweetheart," and then pulled him in for a kiss so passionate that all Felix's objections had melted away with the heat of it.

Once they were seated Mattias didn't waste any time, getting straight to the point. "It has become clear that you require an heir and Felix is not equipped to provide you with one."

Leo's brow creased. "And? The crown will simply pass to the other branch of the family, and my line will end with me." He spoke with utter conviction, and for that alone Felix fell a little bit more in love with him.

"But what if it didn't have to?" Mattias said, a smile playing around his mouth.

"Don't talk in riddles, Mattias. You know it irritates me." Leo leaned back in his chair and propped his boots up on Mattias's desk. Mattias sighed, leaned forward, and shoved his feet off. The look that passed between them told Felix that this was some sort of long-running game.

"Well, if you'll wait just a moment—" There was a knock on the door and Mattias brightened. He walked over and opened the door, waited, then stuck his head out into the corridor and said, "Come in, we won't bite."

A familiar figure stepped into the room, and Felix had to look twice, because he was cleaner than Felix had ever seen him, his thick dark hair combed flat against his head and his cheeks scrubbed pink. Even his boots were clean.

"Your Majesty," Davin squeaked out, biting his lip and

giving a half bow. He was doing his best to mind his manners, and it was clearly taking all his effort. "Mr. Jones said you wanted to see me, Chancellor?"

Mattias patted him on the arm before going and settling himself back in his chair. "Your Majesty, you remember Davin?"

Leo nodded, and there was a long silence while Mattias appeared to be debating something internally before he sighed and said, "There's no way to say this that won't have you arguing, so I suppose the easiest thing would be to show you. Davin, I want you to drop your trousers."

Felix choked on a laugh when Davin's eyebrows drew together and he said, "Begging your pardon, sir, I'm flattered and all, but do we really need an audience?"

Mattias ran his palms down his cheeks and sucked in a long breath. "Gods, you're your father's son, aren't you?" he muttered.

"Wouldn't know, sir. I've never met him," Davin said cheerfully, fumbling the laces on his trousers open and yanking them midway down his thighs, smallclothes and all.

"What's going on, Matty?" Leo demanded. "Why are you stripping my stable boy?"

"Because he's not your stable boy," Mattias said, his grin back in place. "He's your *son*."

"What? I don't have a son!"

"Don't you? Davin, lift your shirttails and turn around." Davin lifted the tails of his shirt, and there, right on his arse cheek, was a small, perfectly formed birthmark —in the shape of a kiss.

Leo's mouth dropped open at the sight, and Felix

would have laughed at his obvious astonishment, if he hadn't been so busy trying to fit all the puzzle pieces together himself. Leo had a *son?*

"I have a son?" Leo said faintly.

"Wait, I'm a prince?" Davin gasped, dropping his shirttails.

"You're King Leopold's son, yes."

Leo tilted his head to the side. "Is your mother Lady Amelia—"

"—Bellefleur, yes, sire."

*"Amelia."* Leo sighed with something like wonder in his voice. "She moved away so suddenly, and I could never find out why. I suppose I know the answer now."

Mattias arched a brow. "The lady in question found herself expecting a blessed event after a certain prince charmed his way into her"—he cast a glance at Davin—"good graces."

"I charm my way into the kitchen girls' good graces all the time," Davin said.

Leo stood and circled Davin, looking him up and down like he was seeing him for the first time, before coming to a stop in front of the boy. "Felix, I have a *son*." He said it with more certainty this time, and the corners of his eyes crinkled with the width of his smile.

"And I'm *royalty,*" Davin agreed, eyes wide. "Wait, does that mean I don't have to shovel shit anymore?"

Mattias chuckled. "Eventually, but for now you have to swear to keep this a secret. Do you understand, Davin? Your anonymity is for your own protection, so you'll stay working for Mother while we decide the best way to introduce you as the prince."

Davin's brow creased, and now that he was looking, Felix could see traces of Leo in the line of his jaw, the dark hair, the stubborn tilt of his chin. "But why do I have to stay in the stables?"

"Remind me why your mother sent you to work here again?" Mattias said.

Davin's shoulders hunched. "Because I have an entitled attitude and no work ethic, but I need one because who knows what life will bring and someday I'll thank her," he recited glumly.

"Quite right, too," Leo said. "Ruling a kingdom is a lot of work." He reached out hesitantly and ruffled Davin's hair.

Davin froze. "Wait, did you say *ruling?*"

Mattias cleared his throat. "It won't be any time soon. But due to recent developments, it does appear you'll be taking the throne in the future."

Davin's grin was pure mischief. "Are the recent developments the king and Felix going at it like rabbits?"

Felix did laugh then.

Like father, like son indeed.

∽

"And you knew this whole time?" Felix asked Mattias.

Once the initial furore had died down, Mattias had suggested that they put their heads together to work out the best way to move forward with revealing Davin's existence, and so Mattias, Leo, and Felix were sitting in Mattias's office. Felix took the chance to ask questions since Leo didn't seem inclined to do much except sit there, smiling to himself.

"I was sworn to secrecy unless the need arose," Mattias said. "The king decided Leo was too young and irresponsible to be burdened with parenthood—and he was right," he added, pointing at Leo, who had stopped grinning long enough to open his mouth. "You were a stroppy little git at seventeen."

"I was *going* to say that my father was wise to do what he did," Leo said, pointing right back at Mattias. "I certainly wasn't ready to be a parent, and Amelia had told me repeatedly that she had no interest in anything more than a fling."

"So what *did* the king do?" Felix asked.

"What royal families have done with unexpected offspring for centuries," Mattias said. "Amelia and her family were more than happy to be awarded a country estate and an income in return for raising the illegitimate son of the prince in safety and seclusion, with the understanding that if it ever came to it, Davin would be informed of his heritage and step up to take the crown."

Felix's nose wrinkled. "So, they just parked the child like a spare carriage to be wheeled out in the case of an accident or emergency? That seems very unfeeling."

"It's not like that," Leo said. "I'm told Davin had quite the pampered existence."

Mattias nodded. "*Too* pampered. It's how he ended up in the stables. I made sure to go and see Amelia twice a year, and last time I visited she was concerned that Davin was showing signs of turning into one of those useless fops who lounge around all day, and she wasn't having it. We decided he needed to try his hand at physical labour and learn some manners. But of course, we couldn't just send him anywhere, so I suggested the stables. I knew Mother wouldn't tolerate his nonsense."

Felix grinned. "So that explains why he was so clueless. I can't *wait* until Mother finds out he's been giving the heir to the throne a clip around the ears. He'll be *mortified*."

"Oh, I don't know," Leo said. "It never stopped him with me."

"You deserved it, though," Mattias said with a laugh.

Leo shrugged. "True. And I do think some more time in the stables will do Davin good before we reveal him as the crown prince."

Felix tilted his head. "How will that work? Won't Davin have to be trained up before you unleash him as your heir?"

Mattias hummed thoughtfully. "Davin's been raised as nobility, so he already knows a lot of the protocols. It's just a matter of educating him in the running of the kingdom, and I'm not sure there's any way to do that other than have him move into the castle and see how it all works. But that won't be for a while. His mother insists he learn how to break a sweat with an honest day's labour first."

"We could be waiting a while in that case," Felix said. "I've never seen someone so eager to avoid work. Although he was improving, so maybe there's hope."

"And he did save your life, love," Leo reminded him, moving to stand behind Felix's chair and kissing the top of his head, "so I think he's already proved himself invaluable."

Felix leaned back and smiled at Leo, who was gazing

down at him with such unabashed fondness that it made Felix's heart clench. He still couldn't believe that they might be able to have this.

Felix forced his attention back to his surroundings when there was a knock at the door. Whoever it was must be important if they hadn't been sent packing by the guard outside. Leo had obviously come to the same conclusion because he called, "Enter!" without checking who it was.

Sophia swept into the room, looking resplendent in a turquoise gown, and breezed over to the table and took a seat. "Hello," she said, addressing Leo. "I hear you have a son, and I'm here to offer my help preparing him to take the throne."

Felix blinked. "How?"

She turned to him, smiling sweetly. "Well, when a prince and woman dally in ways they shouldn't and don't take the necessary precautions, sometimes the woman has a baby. Shall I draw you a picture?"

"I think Felix meant how did you hear about it, ma'am," Mattias said, his lips twitching.

"I've told you, don't call me ma'am. And I happened to see young Davin heading towards the stables, and he was practically skipping, so of course I stopped him and asked him what had him so happy."

"So much for secrecy," Leo muttered.

"In fairness to Davin, he didn't dare not answer, and he did tell me it was a secret." Sophia's smile turned darkly satisfied. "He finds me intimidating, which will work well if I'm going to be teaching him the ins and outs of political intrigue. It means he'll pay attention."

Leo sat back down next to Felix. "I appreciate the offer,

but aren't you returning to Evergreen once the treaty negotiations are over?"

"That's the thing," Sophia said. "I thought I'd stay here. I have"—her unflappable exterior wavered just for a moment before she rallied and looked Leo in the eye—"unfinished business."

Leo's eyebrows rose and a smirk appeared. "Am I right in thinking you're planning to pursue your romantic interest?"

Mattias made a choked noise. "What romantic interest?"

Sophia jutted her chin out. "There's a particular knight who I've developed a deep affection for, and I'm hoping that he'll agree to a betrothal."

Mattias's face fell, his expression the very definition of hangdog. "I see," he said quietly. "Well, whoever this knight is, I hope he's worthy of you, ma'am."

Sophia's eyes sparkled with mischief. "I'm certain he is, although he does seem to suffer from the inability to take a hint."

"Ma'am?"

"It's you, Mattias."

*"Me?"* Felix could see the moment when what Sophia had said sunk in, because Mattias's eyes widened and his face split into a wide smile that had the corners of his eyes creasing attractively. Seeing him like that, Felix couldn't fault the princess for her excellent taste.

"Yes, you. I thought we might wed and then stay here for a year or two while I whip Davin into shape and you teach Felix to manage the king's nonsense."

"I don't have nonsense," Leo said.

"No, you do," Felix said, "and anyway this isn't about you. Matty's getting married!" He paused. "Aren't you?"

Mattias hesitated then stood and took three quick steps until he was standing directly in front of Sophia. He said, "I just need to check one thing first." And with that he put his hands on her waist, pulled her to her feet, and bent down and kissed her. Sophia returned the kiss with enthusiasm, standing on the tips of her toes with her hands tangled in Mattias's hair, and when they parted, they were both wide-eyed and beaming.

"Yes, Sophia," Mattias said, breathless. "I think I should very much like to marry you."

## Epilogue

*Nine months later*

"Are you ready for this?"

Mattias took a deep breath, stopped fidgeting with his cuffs, straightened his spine, and gave a nod. "I've never been more ready for anything in my life."

"Lucky," Leo teased, "seeing as you've had to bring the wedding forward because you couldn't keep it in your trousers."

Mattias grinned, not even slightly repentant. "Sophia was determined to seduce me."

"I doubt she had to try very hard," Leo said with a knowing smile.

"Oh, barely at all. She's very alluring, and I'd be a fool to refuse anything she offers me." Mattias got a dreamy smile on his face, the one he'd often worn since Sophia had decided to claim him as her own.

"Well, it's obvious you're head over heels, and she's lucky to have you."

Mattias's smile widened. "I think I'm the lucky one."

There was a timid tap at the door and a young boy popped his head inside Mattias's chambers. "Begging your pardon, sirs, but Princess Sophia sent me to ask if you were nearly ready, or, um, sorry, sir, but she asked if you'd gotten cold feet and should she start looking for a substitute?"

Mattias laughed. "I'm on my way."

Leo pulled Mattias in for a firm hug and when he stepped back, he said, "I really am happy for you, even if you have to sit through the pomp and ceremony of a royal wedding."

Mattias shrugged. "Sophia's a princess. She deserves a big wedding, and I want to give her the best."

"That seems to be the story of your life now, worshipping your princess."

Mattias's smile was blinding. "I know. Isn't it marvellous?" He clapped Leo on the shoulder and nodded at the door. "Now can you please go so I can get married? I don't want to keep my bride waiting."

∽

Leo took his seat next to Felix, who looked very fine in a white linen shirt with a fitted scarlet jacket and black trousers that hugged the curve of his thighs just so. Felix gave him a warm smile. "How's Matty?"

"Almost bursting with the excitement of it all." Leo bumped their shoulders together, a gentle nudge, and Felix leaned back against him, theirs a comfortable closeness. They settled in to wait for the ceremony to begin.

Soon enough Mattias arrived, followed by a resplendent Sophia, who was swathed in silk as was befitting a princess. The sheer naked affection in her expression when she looked at Mattias as the ceremony started left Leo in no doubt that Mattias was, indeed, a lucky man—but no luckier than Leo was.

Because despite how impossible it should have been, Leo was here with Felix by his side and he'd never been happier. He still ran the kingdom, and he still grumbled at his paperwork, but the difference was that now he had Felix, challenging and encouraging him in equal measure. The relationship between them had only grown stronger in the months that had passed, and waking up every morning with Felix in his bed never failed to thrill him anew.

Of course, the polite fiction in the castle was that Felix stayed close to Leo in his role as Leo's personal guard, but Leo knew for a fact that nobody believed it—not that he cared what anyone thought.

There *were* benefits to being the king, after all.

It probably helped that the previous month Davin had, with much fanfare, been revealed as the crown prince. It was sooner than any of them had expected, but it was as if knowing he was a prince and having a purpose had sparked something within the boy, and he'd shown a remarkable willingness to learn, along with a previously unseen work ethic that had resulted in him being moved out of the stables in a matter of months.

He'd eagerly shadowed both Leo and Mattias around the castle, observing and asking intelligent questions. He'd also won the staff over effortlessly, proving himself to be at least as personable and engaging as his father. When Sophia had taken him under her wing and schooled him in politics, etiquette, and negotiations, he'd listened to her every word with something akin to goddess worship. Overall, he'd taken to castle life, and to the prospect of someday ruling, like a duck to water.

When Sophia had declared that she thought Davin was ready to become a member of the court, Leo had been sceptical. But Sophia, with a gleam in her eye, had issued a challenge. If Davin could complete a successful negotiation, Leo would allow him to claim his birthright.

Leo had agreed, and been equal parts impressed and appalled when Davin had managed, with a combination of easy charm and flawless reasoning, to convince Leo that he should award the coveted parcel of border territory to Sophia—as a wedding gift.

He supposed he really shouldn't have been surprised. Davin was known for sweet-talking the kitchen girls out of their skirts, after all, so a treaty negotiation was probably a piece of cake by comparison, but it *had* convinced him that Davin really was up to the task of ruling.

Leo had announced the existence of Crown Prince Davin Salisbury, heir to the throne of Lilleforth, the following week.

A subtle elbow to the ribs from Felix had Leo turning his attention back to the wedding ceremony. The bishop performing the service droned on and on, and it seemed to take forever, but finally Sophia and Mattias made their vows, both of them damp-eyed and grinning like fools.

Felix reached across and squeezed his hand, and Leo squeezed back, reflecting again on how good life was.

～

"Can we leave yet?" Felix groaned, dragging a hand through his hair as they watched yet another troupe of musicians play yet another tune. The feast had dragged on for long hours, and truthfully Leo was more than ready to leave as well. However, tradition decreed that he stay at least until any visiting royalty had departed, and although most of the guests had left, Sophia's parents had so far shown no signs of going anywhere.

"That depends. Do you really want me to insult King Andros by leaving his daughter's wedding feast before he does?"

Felix's face fell, but a second later a grin appeared on his face. "Oh, but leaving's only an insult if you do it. Me? I can come and go as I please. I'm just the guard. No reason for the king to be offended if I go for a walk and never come back. It's *you* that's stuck here, Your Majesty. Although"—he nodded at the doorway and when Leo turned, he saw King Andros and Queen Ysabel *finally* taking their leave, with Mattias and Sophia following—"perhaps not. No risk of offending anyone now. So, can we leave yet so you can take me to bed? Or have you had too much wine to be of any use to me tonight?"

"You're a brat," Leo said with a huff.

"That's me," Felix agreed cheerfully. "I probably need someone to peel me out of these very well-fitted trousers, put me over their knee, and spank my arse red. And by someone, I mean you." He leaned back in his seat and ran a hand up and down the length of his thigh suggestively.

Those trousers really were criminally tight.

"You *do* need someone to teach you a lesson," Leo said, his blood heating as Felix pressed the heel of his hand against his cock and let out a quiet moan. It was an obvious tease, and more than Leo could bear. "Upstairs, now," he growled, low and urgent. "Strip and wait for me on the bed. And Flick? Get the crop out."

"Yes, *sire*," Felix said breathlessly, eyes wide.

He didn't *quite* bolt out of the room, but it was a close thing, and Leo barely managed to wait a minute before making his excuses and following him.

∽

"You didn't go easy," Felix mumbled into the pillow, his eyes closed. He was naked, legs splayed wide, and he looked utterly ruined.

It suited him.

"No," Leo agreed, smoothing arnica cream over the delicious array of stripes crisscrossing his boy's arse, "I didn't."

"And you fucked me *hard*," Felix continued, arching into Leo's touch when he ran his thumbs up either side of his spine.

"Are you complaining?" Leo asked, knowing very well that he wasn't.

"Not in the least." Felix sighed happily. "But you need

to lie down and hold me now. I'm a poor, delicate creature and I deserve to be coddled."

Leo snorted, but he lay back down on the bed, and Felix wasted no time sprawling across his chest, face pressed against the curve of Leo's shoulder. "Better?" he asked softly, tangling his fingers in Felix's messy mop and kissing the top of his head.

"Mm-hmm," Felix hummed, his weight a solid, comforting presence that Leo could never get enough of.

Leo wrapped an arm around Felix's back, holding him in place. He listened to the crackle of the fireplace and Felix's steady breathing, and he thought about Mattias and how happy he'd looked today exchanging his vows. He thought about the fact that he had a son now, an heir, and wasn't required to produce another one.

And he thought about his charming, irrepressible lover, the man who matched wits with him and refused to be intimidated, and who told him when he was being an arse, but who also rubbed his shoulders after a stressful day and indulged—no, *encouraged*—Leo's bedroom antics.

And he thought about the fact that as king, there was nothing stopping him from making their union binding, if he wished to do so.

"Flick?"

Felix gave a disgruntled huff and lifted his head, blinking sleepily in the candlelight and blowing upward at a stray lock of hair. "Mmm?"

Leo smoothed the hair back. "What would you think about marrying me?"

Felix opened his eyes and stared for a long second, then rolled to one side and propped himself up on one elbow.

"Are you asking because you just had the best sex of your life and you're bathing in the afterglow, or is this a serious question?"

It wasn't quite the response Leo had anticipated, but in fairness, he supposed Felix hadn't been expecting him to ask. "It's a serious question."

"I'd say it's impossible." Felix's voice held a note of wistfulness, though, and Leo, encouraged, sat up and leaned back against the headboard.

"It's not, though. I could issue a royal decree. Kings have done it before in other kingdoms."

Felix bit his lip. "You'd do that?"

"In a heartbeat."

Felix was silent for a moment before asking, "And would it have to be a proper royal wedding?"

"Well, since last I checked I'm still king, yes."

Felix's brow creased, which was less enthusiastic than Leo had been hoping for. "I'd rather not, to be honest. That's not a no," he hastened to add before Leo had time to panic. "I love you to the stars, Leo. But *ye gods,* I don't think I can sit through another royal wedding like today's, even if it *is* my own."

Leo stared at Felix, confused. "You're turning down my proposal because *you don't like the formalities?*"

Felix shrugged. "I'm not turning you down. But I am saying no to a *royal* wedding. The whole thing just seems like such a waste of time, and it creates a lot of extra work for no good purpose. Besides, that bishop loved the sound of his own voice far too much. So I refuse to have anything like that. But if you mean it about wanting to marry me, I'll happily handfast you."

Leo's breath left him in a rush, because this *definitely* wasn't no. "A handfasting? That's what you want?"

"That's what I want. A traditional handfasting, like my parents had. I love you, Leo, but I don't want or need crowds or banquets or musicians and jugglers. I just need you."

When he put it like that, the idea had a certain charm —and a handfasting *was* legally binding, which meant Leo could still have his way on at least one thing.

"Fine. No royal wedding and I'll handfast you, on one condition."

"Oh, we're negotiating now?" Felix eased himself to a sitting position, wincing as his backside came in contact with the bed, and Leo couldn't help the flash of dark satisfaction he felt. It must have shown on his face because Felix caught the expression and rolled his eyes. "Stop looking so pleased with yourself about the state of my arse, and tell me your one condition."

Leo squared his shoulders. "I'd like to appoint you Prince Consort. When you rule at my side, I don't want anyone to doubt that we're on equal footing." He wasn't sure Felix would accept, but he was almost certain he could persuade him. He knew exactly how to make Felix squirm and beg, after all.

But it proved unnecessary. Felix tilted his head, and Leo could see his teeth gleaming in the candlelight as he grinned. "It will take some getting used to, having a title."

"So...is that a yes?"

"Of course it's a yes, my idiot future husband."

"Really?" A wave of sheer, unbridled happiness washed

over Leo, and he couldn't stop the grin spreading across his face.

Felix's answering smile was as bright as a sunrise as he clambered into Leo's lap, setting his knees on either side of him, and surged forward for a kiss. He pulled back long enough to say, "You're just fortunate that I love you enough that I'll tolerate a bollocksy title." And then he went back to kissing Leo with a hunger that held the promise of much, much more.

And right now, with his lover—no, his *future husband*—sitting in his lap and kissing him passionately, Leo had to agree.

He was the most fortunate man alive.

# Afterword

Thank you for reading The King's Delight. If you enjoyed this book, please consider taking a moment to leave a review on Amazon, Goodreads, or your social media platform of choice.

# About the Author

Sarah started life in New Zealand. She came to Australia for a working holiday, loved it, and never left. She lives in Western Australia with her partner, two cats, two dogs and a life-size replica TARDIS.

She spends half her time at a day job and the rest of her time reading and writing about clueless men falling in love, with a dash of humour and spice thrown in along the way.

Her proudest achievements include having adult kids who will still be seen with her in public, the ability to make a decent sourdough loaf, and knowing all the words to Bohemian Rhapsody.

She has co-authored both the Bad Boyfriends, Inc and the Adventures in Aguillon series with Lisa Henry. Socially Orcward, the third book in the Aguillon series, was runner up in the Best Asexual Book category in 2021's Rainbow Awards.

You can follow her on Amazon, Instagram, Goodreads, Facebook and Bookbub. She shares a Facebook group with

Lisa Henry and JA Rock, The Book Nook, where you'll find news of latest projects, giveaways, and plenty of pet pictures.

You can find Sarah's website at sarahhoneyauthor.com

*Also by Sarah Honey*

*With Lisa Henry*

*Adventures in Aquillon*
Red Heir (Adventures in Aguillon, Book 1)
Elf Defence (Adventures in Aguillon, Book 2)
Socially Orcward (Adventures in Aguillon, Book 3)

*Bad Boyfriends, Inc*
Awfully Ambrose (Bad Boyfriends, Inc. Book 1)
Horribly Harry (Bad Boyfriends, Inc, Book 2)
Terribly Tristan (Bad Boyfriends, Inc, Book 2)

*Standalone*
Cool Story, Bro